WITHDRAWN

The
Safest
Lie

The Safest Lie

ANGELA CERRITO

Holiday House / New York

Copyright © 2015 by Angela Cerrito
All Rights Reserved
HOLIDAY HOUSE is registered in the U.S. Patent and Trademark Office.
Printed and Bound in June 2015 at Maple Press, York, PA. USA.
www.holidayhouse.com
First Edition
1 3 5 7 9 10 8 6 4 2
"To the Young" by Adam Asnyk. English translation by Jarosław Zawadski

Library of Congress Cataloging-in-Publication Data
Cerrito, Angela.
The safest lie / by Angela Cerrito. — First edition.
pages cm
Summary: A nine-year-old Jewish girl, helped by Irena Sendler and the Zegota
organization, is smuggled out of the Warsaw ghetto, given a new identity,
and sent to live in the countryside for the duration of World War II.
ISBN 978-0-8234-3310-0 (hardcover)
1. Holocaust, Jewish (1939–1945)—Poland—Juvenile fiction.
2. Jews—Poland—Juvenile fiction.   3. World War, 1939–1945—
Underground movements—Poland—Juvenile fiction.
[1. Holocaust, Jewish (1939–1945)—Poland—Fiction.
2. Jews—Poland—Fiction.
3. World War, 1939–1945—Underground movements—Poland—Fiction.
4. Identity—Fiction.   5. Poland—History—Occupation, 1939–1945—Fiction.]
I. Title.
PZ7.C3193Saf 2015
[Fic]—dc23
2014028428

To Mom and Mike

Acknowledgments

There are three people I must thank first and foremost. Kathleen Ahrens, the number one person responsible for insisting this book leave my hard drive; Caitlin Blaisdell, who took me under her wing and guided me until Anna's story was ready to venture out into the world; and Julie Amper, editor extraordinaire and also a patient teacher. I can't thank the three of you enough for all that you have taught me and for your unwavering enthusiasm for Anna's story.

I received a tremendous amount of support in researching this novel. In 2005, I was awarded the Kimberly Colen Memorial grant by the Society of Children's Book Writers and Illustrators, SCBWI. I would like to thank the family of Kimberly Colen and the grant committee, Marvin Terban, Karen Terban and Caron Lee Cohen. The grant made it possible for me to travel to Warsaw, Poland, for research. The Jewish Historical Institute in Warsaw provided access to archives. Juergen Hensel and Mrs. Agnieska Reszka assisted with the research. Ana Mieszkowska, Irena Sendler's biographer, agreed to several interviews and offered endless insight. Ewa Prokop is an extraordinarily dedicated translator who spent full days assisting me in Warsaw, followed by months—and then years—of email correspondence. Alicja Karnas, film producer Mary Skinner and Dr. Kaya Mirecka, director of the Polish Center in Washington, DC, introduced me to research contacts in Warsaw. Ana Mahloch, who was a young teacher in Warsaw at the time, invited me to stay in her home. Dr. Ilana Abramovitch gave me a behind-the-scenes look as well as valuable advice during my research at the Museum of Jewish History in New York. Julian Volj, Michlean L. Amir and Leo Greenbaum answered my research questions. Irena Sendler graciously offered me her time, shared her memories and was enthusiastic and supportive when I met with her in Warsaw. She continued to encourage me after I arrived home. I cherish the time I spent with Irena, and I'm certain her influence will continue to motivate and inspire me throughout my life.

Thank you to everyone at Holiday House, not only for your publishing expertise, but for inviting me to be part of the Holiday House family! Thanks also to George Newman's careful eye and to Francois Thisdale for the beautiful and emotional cover.

I will always be grateful to Steve and Laura Butler, two of the most amazing pay-it-forward people anyone could ever meet. Thank you both for your support and your ever-impressive, gobsmacking awesomeness. Earlier versions of this manuscript were read by Jeanne Litt and Linda Covella. Thank you for your time, suggestions and encouragement. Speaking of encouragement, Esther Hershenhorn was there every step of the way!

I attended Polish-language lessons at the Millennium Language School in Roveredo, Italy, in preparation for my research trip. Their staff, along with Ewa Prokop, assisted in translation of Polish texts. Norma Klein spent many weekend hours with me, translating an entire book from German to English. Grandma's sayings were found on the website of Kehilat Israel in Lansing, Michigan. Thanks to Stephen Rayburn, webmaster, for the many hours of work creating and maintaining the project. Yiddish sayings were reviewed by Anna Levine and Dr. Alexander Levine. Any mistakes with language translations are my own. I would also like to thank Jarek Zawadski for giving permission for the use of his translation of Adam Asnyk's poem *To the Young* found at the end of this book.

Verla Kay and all the moderators of the Blue Board have created an amazing place for writers to learn, bond and grow. If it were possible to live anywhere in cyberspace, I would choose Verla's!

Wayne Talley and Udo Geier deserve special mention. Wayne was over-the-moon enthusiastic after reading the first draft of this novel so many years ago. Udo frequently asked to read it as well. I waited, because the manuscript wasn't ready. Back then, I wasn't aware of how little time we had left. Dad and Udo, you inspire me. I miss you both every day.

The Cochran family, Kimberly, Todd, Jack and Grant, were the first to hear a reading of this version of the novel. Christine Beshara never fails to open her home to me, providing the most perfect writing escape/vacation I could ever hope for.

Mom and Mike, this one is for you. Actually, as I'm sure you know, they are all for you.

If you are still reading this, you are most likely related to me. I am blessed with a large and supportive extended family. It would be nearly impossible to list everyone by name. So to my large (and growing) enthusiastic, fun, wonderful relatives, an enormous THANK YOU.

And most of all, I am forever grateful to Terry, Alexandria and Samantha, who are my everything.

Chapter I

Mama's arm is draped over me, soft as a butterfly's wing. Papa clears his throat and pats at his coat pockets. He's been awake all night guarding us from the two men who arrived yesterday. I fling my hand in front of my face and peek through my fingers. The men are arguing. They don't speak Polish or German or French. I can't understand their language, but I feel their words stomping on top of each other, hard and heavy, like soldiers' boots.

Papa pats his pockets again. It worries Mama when he does this. "Makes it look like you have something worth stealing," she tells him. There is nothing left to steal. My silver hair brush and Papa's leather belt were taken two days ago. Or three days ago.

Mama's sleeping snug in her winter coat, so Papa can pat his pockets all he wants and it won't upset her. His pockets crunch where he touches them; they're stuffed with newspaper, nothing worth stealing. Anyone can find newspaper blowing down the street or covering a sleeping person or spread over a body.

Mama complains to Papa about the newspapers every day. "Why are you always picking up newspaper?"

"This one is clean, a nice clean sheet," Papa answers. He folds each piece of newspaper very small and tucks them away, deep in his pockets.

I don't save newspapers, but I understand. It's nice to have something, anything, to put in your pocket when all you own in the world are the clothes you are wearing.

Mama jerks awake and pulls me into a quick hug before sitting up. She gives the new men a hard look and they stop arguing for a long moment to stare back at her. Mama waves her arms for me to stand up and insists Papa lie down. He stretches out on the mat with his shoes hanging off the edge.

I rub my eyes and run a finger across my teeth. Mama circles our half of the room, unbuttons her coat and buttons it back again. Mama has only letters in her pocket, three long letters from Grandma. It isn't cold enough to wear a winter coat, but keeping it on is the only way to prevent it from getting snatched away. Mama runs her fingers through my hair, pulling apart the tangles. Papa's snoring before she's finished.

I straighten my clothes. Dirt outlines my fingernails and fills the wrinkles of my knuckles. Mama puts a hand on each of my shoulders and closes her eyes, something she does every morning. I wish I could look into her thoughts. I ask the question I've wanted to ask for weeks. "Why do you close your eyes like that?"

"Oh, Anna . . ." She looks away, surprised I noticed. Or surprised I asked. "It's nothing. I . . . make a picture in my mind of you at home, in your school uniform, starting a . . . normal day."

My stomach spins and wobbles, but not because I'm hungry. Mama's words erase these two years. I long for my school uniform hanging on the peg behind my door, my own room, Papa's carpentry shop, the apple tree in our yard . . . more apples than I could eat in a season. Warm white bread . . . so much bread, I dropped it from the bridge to share with the ducks.

My stomach twirls and bends, stretches as if it can reach into the past and take the food I left there. Memories of home always circle around to food.

Chapter 2

Now that there are strangers in our room, Mama can't walk me to Mrs. Rechtman's youth circle. "There is no need to worry," Mama says. These are the words she uses when danger creeps in close. "We don't know these men yet. I can't leave your father asleep and alone." I carry her voice in my head, warning me of other dangers. I walk slowly down the steps. *Don't draw attention to yourself, Anna.* And keep my hands off the rails. *Germs are everywhere, Anna.*

Mrs. Rechtman nods as each child takes a seat on the ground. I don't see Halina so I sit near the front, next to a girl I haven't met. Sonia rushes into the yard and recites a handful of names to Mrs. Rechtman. Sonia is fifteen. She has long dark hair and eyes so dark they are almost black. She is always helping.

I study the group this morning: only seven boys and five girls, including me. There used to be almost one hundred children at youth circle. But that was two years ago when we first moved here. Two years ago each family had their own apartment and enough food to survive.

We even had a secret school. Mrs. Rechtman taught in an abandoned basement. Halina and I sat in the center of the first row. We came early each day because it was our job to set the books at each desk before the other students arrived. Mrs. Rechtman had so many books, hidden in tall stacks behind the cabinets along the back wall.

3

Two years ago, even when the ghetto walls were built up high and the gates were closed and guarded, we had everything: a secret school, enough food, our own home. And there weren't so many people dying.

Mrs. Rechtman stands up on her rock and forces a smile. "We have a great deal of work today."

Halina rushes in and squeezes beside me. Her brother, Marek, barefoot, stands off to the side. Mrs. Rechtman gives us instructions: there is clothing to be distributed, messages to deliver, but no food. Just as we are about to split into groups, Mrs. Rechtman stops talking and sits down. She puts her head in her hands and we all freeze. Our ears reach for the sounds of soldiers' boots. Should I run? Or try to hide?

Mrs. Rechtman sobs. She's been sobbing on and off for days, since they took her husband and daughter.

It's quiet. No soldiers are stomping or talking. But a shadow stretches into our courtyard between the buildings. Sonia walks toward it.

"Jolanta!" Sonia's voice is soft but we all hear it and let out our breath. The cold hand grabbing my heart melts away. There's no reason to be afraid.

Jolanta isn't tall. But she's standing and Mrs. Rechtman is still sitting on her rock. When she pulls Mrs. Rechtman into a hug, it looks like Jolanta is the mother and Mrs. Rechtman is her daughter. Jolanta walks Mrs. Rechtman away from us. Sonia takes charge. I'm put in the group to distribute donated clothing. We stare at the mismatched shirts and trousers. I try to convince myself that it isn't pointless to donate clothing to people who are starving. Sonia reads our expressions. "It isn't too soon to prepare for winter."

Mrs. Rechtman calls us all back to the circle. "Jolanta has good news for us. Homework for each of you to share with your families." Homework is food. *Food!* My mind explodes with food dreams: meat, plums, carrots. I wonder if I'll remember what meat tastes like if I ever get a chance to eat it again.

"Only a small amount of homework. And something else." She pauses and looks at Jolanta, but Jolanta is quiet, as usual. "Three vaccinations against typhoid fever for three children in our circle. Who will it be? How will we decide?" Mrs. Rechtman's eyes are dry now; they're not even red.

A tall boy stands up. "I nominate Sonia. She is the hardest worker. Everyone knows it."

Everyone agrees. Except Sonia, of course.

"And the other two?" Mrs. Rechtman looks around.

I swallow the lump in my throat and stand. "I nominate Halina and Marek."

"We can't just pick our friends," a boy objects.

"It's true Halina is my friend." I take a deep breath to help make my words strong. "I nominate her and Marek for good reasons. Both of their parents have the fever. They have two little sisters to care for. Does anyone else have the disease in their home?"

No one speaks up.

"Then Halina and Marek are the most at risk. They come to youth circle and work every day. They should be given the vaccinations."

We vote. The immunizations go to Sonia, Halina and Marek. We make a tight circle around them and watch as they have needles poked into their arms and the lifesaving medicine pushed into their bodies.

Jolanta's eyes land on me when she finishes the last injection. "What is your name?"

"Anna Bauman."

"And why did you ask for your friends and not yourself?"

"They are a better choice. They can care for their parents and younger sisters. I'm an only child." Jolanta nods. I can feel her eyes on me as I make my way to the mismatched clothes.

With the promise of homework, we quickly pull on three or four shirts and one or two extra pairs of pants and set out delivering the clothes. At the end of the day I have four cabbage leaves, three pieces of dried fruit and a half slice of acorn bread tied in my scarf. Jolanta stays with us later than usual and shocks me by asking to walk me home.

"Do you speak German?" She slows her pace next to me, her head in constant motion, scanning the streets.

"Of course."

Jolanta switches to German. "Tell me how old you are and if you have any relatives living outside the ghetto."

"Nine. My aunt lives in Canada. She's too far away to help. My father has tried. The rest of our family is in Lodz, the Lodz ghetto." I swallow and try to push down the lump in my throat, remembering Grandma's letters. "At least we think they are still there."

"I'd like to meet your parents." Jolanta switches back to Polish as we pass three boys leaning up against the wall of my building.

"I'm sure they would like to meet you too." Jolanta. She smells like clean clothes and grassy fields and she brings us the greatest treasures—dried fruit and bread and cabbage leaves, and today, magic medicine.

I avoid the handrails and so does Jolanta. I almost don't feel the steps under my feet; I am bubbling with excitement as we make our way up the steps to my door.

Chapter 3

Jolanta, Mama and Papa whisper together. I know they are whispering about me. Papa's voice rises. "No, I won't hear of it." He takes a step back. Mama ducks her head in closer to Jolanta's and continues the conversation.

When we lived at home, Papa always had the final say, about everything. He drapes an arm around my shoulder and pulls me to the small window under the slanted ceiling. During our first nights here, Papa and I looked out the window together. As we watched the walls around our block grow taller and taller, he insisted the war would be over soon. He sounded like a leader on the radio. "Poland will never stop fighting, Anna. The country is young, but the people are old, centuries old. One hundred and twenty-three years Poland was absent from the map. Then back again. Nothing can stop the Polish people."

Now he's silent, his head nearly touching the streaked glass. I know Papa's trying to look out past the guards and the gates. Maybe he's hoping to see his old shop with the stacks of wood outside, machines humming inside and a storage room of new furniture waiting to be delivered. Like Mama with her eyes closed resting her hands upon my shoulders each morning and Papa at the window searching, I remember too. Our old life is only a few blocks away and not so long ago.

Too soon, we are spotted. "Alms, alms," cries a girl beneath our window. "Alms! Alms! Bread! Please, bread!" A crowd of orphan children gathers below. I close my eyes and back away, clutching my scarf with the precious food inside.

The two men who share our room stare at me with hungry eyes as if they can see the food hidden beneath the cloth. I want to be kind. I want to share. I know I am fortunate to have a mother and father. We are lucky to have a room, even if we must share with strangers. And today we have food. Thanks to Jolanta.

Jolanta leaves without a smile or a nod. "Do you remember, I told you about her?" I ask Mama. "Isn't she amazing?"

Mama folds me into a hug. "More amazing that you can imagine," she says.

We wait in line for the bathroom at the end of the hall and the three of us enter together. It is the only place that gives us a little bit of safety and privacy to do something dangerous— eat. I place my scarf in Mama's hands. After Papa blesses it, we each chew on a piece of dried fruit, making it last as long as possible. Papa quickly blesses the cabbage leaves; his eyes are on the door. Mama insists I have two cabbage leaves, while they each have only one.

"The bread is for you, Anna," Mama says.

"I can't eat it all."

"Yes," Papa agrees. "You must."

It's always this way. Mama says that I need more food because I'm growing and Papa agrees with her every time. I bless the bread. "Blessed are you, Lord our God, King of the universe, who brings forth bread from the earth."

My parents fix their eyes on me, making sure I swallow every crumb. When I'm finished, they nod as if I've just completed my homework and done a good job on it too.

The next morning, before sunrise, there is a knock. Mama jumps out of bed and flies to the door. I see Jolanta's face as Mama cracks it open. She passes Mama a small piece of paper and disappears. Mama leans back against the closed door. She doesn't know that one of the men has woken up. He watches her. She doesn't know that I've got one eye closed and the other eye fixed on her face. She unfolds the paper, brings it up to her mouth and gives it a kiss. I quickly shut my spying eye before she climbs into bed and lies down next to me.

Chapter 4

This morning the two men leave early. They take all of their belongings: two big packs that they haven't opened, a rolled blanket and a pillowcase. I've seen them take a book, a comb and a pair of shoes from the pillowcase, but nothing else. The room feels bigger, but we don't step into the empty space. Even though every trace of them is gone, that half of the room is assigned to them.

When Mama's untangling my hair, she tells me I won't be going to youth circle.

"I have to. I need to help." It's a quiet morning; there's been no gunfire, no sign of a raid.

"Not today, Anna." She taps my cheek and I turn my head to the light from the small window.

I hate the dangerous days. The days we must stay inside our room or rush off to one of the hiding places. "Please, Mama. There might be homework. There's no sign of danger."

I know as soon as the words slip out that I've made a mistake. Mama always says danger is everywhere. But she surprises me and agrees. "You're right, there's no sign of danger." She lifts a new strand of my hair. "I have work for you here today."

"Yes, Mama." She didn't say homework, so I know it's not food. But what work could I do in our room? We've already rolled up the mat. Papa's standing by the dirty window. We have no cleaner or rags to clean with, no broom to sweep the floor.

Mama taps my other cheek and I turn my head. If this were a real school day, back home, Mama would pull my hair tight and twist it into braids. Then she'd tie them at the ends with red or gold ribbons to match my school uniform.

When she's finished with my hair, she closes her eyes like she always does. She's thinking about home. I try to block out the picture of our old house, of Grandma and my cousins. Instead, I think of Sonia, already busy at work outside, and Halina and Marek, strong and healthy because of the shot they had yesterday. I should be helping them.

Mama pulls my hand. "Let's sit." She sits on the floor with her back to the wall and I sit beside her. "Today, Anna, you have a new name."

"My name is Anna."

"Right," Mama says. "Your name is Anna. But, starting today, it's not Anna Bauman. It's Anna Karwolska."

Papa turns from the window. "What have you done? I said I didn't want this."

Mama tilts her chin up at Papa. "It's going to happen," she says. "It's going to happen." She looks at me. "Your name is Anna Karwolska. Tell me your name."

I glance at Papa. His shoulders slump and he moves back to the window.

Mama taps my leg. "Say it."

"My name is Anna Karwolska." The words are heavy and far away, like a stone thrown so far out into the lake that it is impossible to hear the splash.

I quickly learn a new name, address, birthday and the names of Anna Karwolska's parents. I even learn her parents' birthdays. Mama switches to French and asks the same questions over and over. And then in German, she makes me repeat the new name and all of the information again and again.

It takes concentration to remember every detail, to answer Mama's questions quickly and perfectly.

Papa turns away from the window and looks down at us.

"How old are you?" Mama asks me in German.

"*Acht.*" Eight, I answer, though I'm really nine. Anna Karwolska is still eight. "Now may I go to youth circle? I know all the answers."

Mama shakes her head. "Yes, you know the answers, but you must speak every word like you believe it. Make me believe it."

How can I make her believe so many lies? One of Grandma's sayings comes to me and I blurt it out without thinking. "The truth is in sight. The lie is behind the eyes."

Mama locks her eyes on me and responds with another favorite saying of Grandma's. "The truth has many faces." Then she sighs and says, "Please only Polish or German. Not Yiddish; it's too dangerous."

Only Jewish people speak Yiddish. When I was three years old, I used to call it Grandma's language because everyone spoke to Grandmother in Yiddish. I take a breath and prepare to answer more of Mama's questions, but we are interrupted by a light knock on the door. Everyone knocks lightly, so the people inside know it's not a soldier at the door. Papa opens it and Halina rushes in. Marek follows his sister like a shadow.

Halina greets my parents. When she turns to me, she begins to sob.

"What is it? What's wrong?"

"Jolanta said she could help Mrs. Rechtman escape. She has papers and a safe house outside the ghetto."

I want to sob too, to stomp my foot like I did when I was small. I wish I could yell *No! No! No! No!* But it is impossible for me to raise my voice. I know I can't draw attention to myself. That's one way people get killed. Halina's sobs are quiet. Her tears soak into my shirt.

If Mrs. Rechtman leaves, we will be miserable. My mind leaps over the guards and outside the gate. Jolanta can do anything. She sneaks food and medicine into the ghetto and she can sneak things—people—out. Mrs. Rechtman will have food. She will be safe. Halina wipes her face. I put my hand on her shoulder. "Don't cry. It's for the best," I tell Halina. "When will she leave?" I worry for a moment that I've missed her, missed my chance to say good-bye.

Halina shakes her head. "She won't go. She told Jolanta that she won't leave until all of the children are safe."

Of course, Mrs. Rechtman would never leave us.

When Halina leaves, Mama unrolls the mat. Two years ago, when I lived at home, I was too big for naps, but here everything is different. I don't mind. Sometimes sleep can take away the feeling of being hungry.

Even while I am asleep, Mama shakes my shoulder and asks, "What is your name?"

"Anna."

"Anna who?"

By the third time, I answer her without hesitating: "Anna Karwolska."

Chapter 5

In three days Mama has her wish. I am able to be Anna Karwolska all day. It is as automatic as saying my prayers.

I wake from a deep sleep, uncomfortable. Not from sleeping on the floor or Mama lying beside me, I'm used to that. It's because Papa's leaning against the wall with his eyes glued on me tightly, as if I'll disappear if he looks away.

I sit up and stare real hard back at him. When he sees I'm fully awake, Papa holds out his hand. I take it and stand. He barely glances at the sleeping strangers in our room as we walk to the window. I lean into Papa and we stare up at the moon. I put my hand on the cool window and Papa surprises me by tracing his finger around it.

He surprises me again by speaking in a calm whisper. It's a poem.

> *"The brightening flame of truth pursue,*
> *Seek to discover ways no human knows.*
> *With every secret now revealed to you,*
> *The soul of man expands within the new."*

Papa talks on and on. I don't understand it all, but I love the way his voice, so quiet, fills the room. The final line is about stars fading into the night. Papa's voice, still quiet, is strong, strong enough to climb into the sky and whisper to the stars.

Chapter 6

The men who share our room leave early each morning. They stay out all day and only return in the evening to sleep. But we know they could show up at any time. Papa surprises us by saying he is going for a walk. He hardly leaves the room anymore.

Papa returns a short time later with a carrot. He leans his back against the door because it doesn't lock. We silently pass the carrot around, each of us taking one bite. Mama barely scrapes the carrot against her teeth. I look to Papa. He always insists that she eat. But I catch him doing the same thing. The way he scrapes the carrot sounds like a bite, but there is very little for him to chew. I take a small bite and pass the carrot to Mama again.

I know about surviving in the ghetto. And I know about people who try to get out. They need fake papers, fake names, entire fake identities. Mama wants me to be Anna Karwolska, but she hasn't told me when we will leave or where we will go.

"If I'm Anna Karwolska, are you her mother? Is Papa her father?"

"I know all about Anna Karwolska's mother," Mama says. "And your father knows all there is to know about her father."

The carrot is back around to me again. "But *are* you her mother? *Is* Papa her father?" I take another small bite.

Papa holds the carrot in his hand. I study the small scar on the side of his finger. Mama nudges him to eat. "It's not time to talk about this, Anna." Her voice is low. "It will be time, soon enough."

There is a light tap on the door. "Open your mouth, Anna." Papa holds out the last bit of carrot to me. I do as he says and he pops it into my mouth. Papa opens the door.

Jolanta steps in. Without a greeting, she places a package wrapped in brown paper in Mama's hands. She looks at Papa and says, "I will need every address. Use the inside of the paper packaging."

Papa holds out his hands, helpless. Jolanta nods and pulls two sharp pencils from her coat pocket. Papa's eyes widen as he stares at the pencils in his palm. I can't remember the last time I saw a pencil. Perhaps in Mrs. Rechtman's school, so long ago. At home, Papa always had a pencil in his hand and usually wore one over each ear as well. When we first moved to the ghetto we had a big box full of pencils and a shelf full of books and a kitchen table with four chairs and an oven and . . .

To Mama, Jolanta says only one word, "Hurry!" before she dashes out the door.

Mama tucks the package under her coat out of sight and takes me by the hand. We walk four blocks and turn up the walkway to Anton's house. Anton used to help Papa make furniture. His wife answers Mama's tap at the door. Anton is soon at her side. The house is packed with people.

Mama offers him two carrots for a basin of water. We follow Anton deep into the house, down a long hallway. One or two families are crowded into each room. At the end of the hall is a small bathroom without any fixtures. A pipe sticks out of the wall where there once was a sink. There is a hole where the toilet used to be. Mama hands over the two carrots, and in a short while Anton's wife brings us a big bowl of cold water and a cloth. Mama closes the door and hands me the wet cloth. I drape it over my face, tilting my head up, and stop to enjoy the moment.

"Hurry, Anna," Mama urges. Though there isn't any soap,

the wet cloth erases the dirt and dust from my skin like magic. For the first time in weeks, my arms, my legs, even my hair feels clean and light. When I finish, Mama says, "Get dressed quickly and be sure to cover your hair with your scarf."

Back in our room, Mama bites the material at the bottom of her shirt and tears off two small strips of cloth. Papa stands with his back to the window, watching as she pulls my hair into two tight braids and ties them with the strips of faded pink material. Mama unwraps the package from Jolanta. Inside is a new school uniform. My hands reach out to stroke the dark blue skirt. It has been so long since I've seen something so new or so clean. Mama looks up at Papa. "She must get dressed quickly."

Papa takes the brown paper and leaves the room. I slip into the new clothes. The shirt is so new and stiff, I have to force each button through its hole. The uniform is big and long; I feel like I'm wearing a costume. I stick my feet into my shoes as Mama opens the door for Papa. He takes one look at me and folds me into his arms.

He shows Mama the lists of names and addresses he's written for Jolanta. "I need the address in Lodz," he says.

Mama's hand goes to her pocket. She pulls out Grandma's letter, takes a pencil from Papa and hands both to me. "Anna, your grandmother has printed the return address here on the envelope. Copy it, letter for letter, right here." She points to the bottom of the brown paper.

I nod and sit down on the floor to write. Grandma's printing is much neater than her handwriting. I can understand her letters. It has been months since I held a pencil, but I write *Lodz, Wolborska 24* under my grandfather's name. It almost makes me happy. As though they will see the writing and know it is from me.

"Last word," says Mama, pointing to Grandma's address.

I nod, bite my bottom lip and print *getto* below the street name. For a moment I can't find my breath. My grandparents, my aunts and uncles, my cousins . . . Jakub. They are not only far away, but in a ghetto. Just like us.

I give the pencil and paper to Mama, but keep Grandma's letter. It is the first one she sent to us. "Please, may I read it?"

Mama is silent, surprised. I don't like reading Grandma's letters. The first is all bad news. The other two are even worse. Still, I unfold the thin papers and steady my eyes on Grandma's scribbles. Her handwriting makes some letters pointed where they should be curved. In a few moments, my eyes adjust and I can read Grandma's writing as easily as the words in my first reader.

This letter is about my grandparents leaving their home. I read how they were forced to leave everything: their furniture, their dishes, their horses and even their old dog, Felek.

I stand and give the letter back to Mama. Papa hugs me once again. As soon as he lets go, Mama kneels in front of me. "Your name is Anna Karwolska."

"I know."

"Your parents are dead."

"What?"

"Your parents, Anna Karwolska's parents, are dead."

My throat tightens as if I've swallowed a stone. Papa's face burns red. "Is this necessary? Must you be so harsh?"

Mama stands to face him. She places her hands on her hips and for a second she looks bigger. I see a flash of Mama from before we moved into the ghetto, before she grew so thin and so pale. "This is nothing," she says to Papa. "I must be even harsher." Mama's eyes lock onto mine. "Most important, you are not Jewish."

"Yes I am."

"You are *Anna Karwolska*. Anna Karwolska is not Jewish. Say it. Say, 'I am not Jewish.' "

The words taste rotten on my tongue but I whisper, "I am not Jewish." If only Mama would hug me, the way Papa did. If she would just tell me that I am doing a good job.

"Always remember, you must never admit that you are Jewish. Do you understand?"

I nod.

"Anna Karwolska hates Jewish people. She would never play with a Jewish child. She would never help a Jewish adult. Say it. Say, 'I hate all Jews.' "

"Mother, no!"

"Your mother is dead. Say it. Say, 'I hate all Jews.' " Mama's voice is like a growl.

I take a step back. "No."

"Say it."

"You're not my mother. You can't make me say anything." My body feels cold and heavy and far away.

"I love you," says Mama, my real live mother, Anna Bauman's mother. Mama blinks back tears. "I only want you to be safe."

I step forward and Mama's arms tighten around me. They aren't light like butterfly wings. They're strong, the strongest thing in the world.

Chapter 7

Someone taps on the door three times. Before Papa can answer it, the door opens. Jolanta sticks her head inside and says, "Be ready." The door closes quickly and silently.

Mrs. Rechtman visits next. Her eyes dance between Mama and Papa. She nods to me. "You look very nice, Anna." Mrs. Rechtman turns to Papa next. "I have to take her now."

I've known from the start that learning to be Anna Karwolska was preparing to leave. But now Mama's words come back to me. *Your parents are dead.* This can't be right. I look up at Mama. "You're not coming with me?" She stares deep into my eyes as if she can see something more—more than me. But she's silent. "You and Papa, you're not coming with me?"

Mrs. Rechtman says it again. "I have to take her now."

Something in my brain screams, "*No!*" My shoes are frozen to this spot, to this room I share with Mama and Papa. Mama's arms are around me again. She seems to stretch big enough to swallow me whole. Papa reaches his arms out. All that's left of me for him to grasp are my hands. He's got a tight hold to them as if he'll never let me go.

I can't hear my shouts over the cries of my parents. Mrs. Rechtman pulls their arms away and separates me from Mama and Papa. In the next instant, I am out the door.

I'm not crying. But I'm not breathing either. My chest is so tight, it hurts to breath. Mrs. Rechtman tosses a dirty smock over my head to hide the new school uniform. "Be silent. Stay close to me."

She hurries down the stairs and out into the crowd. People bump and push against each other on the streets, but I stay right on her heels, letting no one between us. On and on we walk. Mrs. Rechtman seems to gain speed with every step she takes. She doesn't look back.

There is no end to the number of children begging for bread. Round eyes and open hands reach out to me as I go by. I think of Halina; I didn't say good-bye. One small boy is holding a sock. He waves it at me as I pass. "Bread, please. Bread." I've seen children begging on the street before, but I had no idea there were so many.

A mother stands with her two girls. Their voices sing out to me, "Bread? Bread? Bread?"

Mrs. Rechtman stops in front of a large brick building. People flow in and out of the doors, like river water swirling between rocks. Mrs. Rechtman bends to face me. "Stay by my side and don't make a sound. When someone takes your hand, go. Don't speak. Stay quiet. Do you understand?"

I nod, afraid to make a sound.

Mrs. Rechtman pulls the smock off and tosses it away. It's snatched up by a street child before it hits the ground. I turn to look, but the boy or girl has disappeared down the road.

Mrs. Rechtman rests a hand on my shoulder and we flow with the crowd into the building. The entry room is as large as the theater near my old house. It's crowded with people and conversations. Everyone walks past us. It is as if I don't exist.

There's a quick tug on my hand, and my feet immediately move to follow a lady with short dark hair. We walk together to the end of a narrow hallway. She opens a door and motions me inside. I realize it's a closet. "Wait here. I will bring you to my office and hide you under my desk. I will only have a minute, so when I open the door, come quickly."

She closes the door and I am surrounded by darkness. I didn't get a good look at the room before the door closed. I don't remember how crowded it is. I stare at the place where the door will open, and stand up straight. I don't dare move or even lean; I could bump into something. I wonder how long it will take for the lady to return. *Please, please come soon,* I pray.

I try to be ready to leave quickly. What I will do if the lady doesn't come back? Then I have a more frightening thought: what if someone else opens the door?

Chapter 8

When the door finally opens, the light stings my eyes. I blink a couple of times to be sure the lady standing in front of me is the same woman who hid me. I know for certain when she whispers, "Hurry."

The woman stands in the hall. Her head scans back and forth like a child waiting to cross a busy street. She tugs my arm. In just two steps we are across the hall, standing in a room full of furniture.

"This is my desk. Quick, underneath." I crawl into the space, fold my knees under my chin and lean against the cool wood. "Stay put," says the woman. She sits in her chair and scoots forward.

Of course, I'll stay put. Where would I go?

In a few minutes, the door begins to open and close. The office fills with the buzz of people working. None of them know I am here.

Anna Karwolska! From the moment I left home, I hadn't once thought about being Anna Karwolska. Without Mama's questions it slipped my mind completely. Now, more than ever, I must keep Anna Karwolska first in my mind. I must become Anna Karwolska.

People move about the room. Some talk. Some even laugh. But the lady with the short dark hair doesn't budge. I spell my new name over and over again. I remember my birthday and my parents' birthdays and my address in a town far away. I try to imagine Anna Karwolska's city, her school and her friends. But I get all mixed up with my own school and friends, my life before we moved to the ghetto.

The woman's hand reaches under the desk. It holds a piece of bread, a full piece of bread. I take it silently. It's real brown bread, not acorn bread. I smell it and my mouth instantly waters. I break the bread into four pieces and put them in my pocket. But bread this soft is too difficult to resist. I select a piece, pull the crust off. It is too dangerous to whisper. Instead, I recite the blessing in my mind and imagine myself speaking loudly and clearly. I eat the crust in tiny bites that melt in my mouth.

I wish I could share some with Mama and Papa.

The sounds in the office quiet down. The door opens and closes repeatedly. Throughout it all, the lady stays seated. When the office is finally silent, the lady bends down. "Wait here. There are windows in this room, so you must stay under the desk. Someone will come for you."

Who will come? And when?

The woman moves away and there's more room under the desk. I change positions for the first time since I crawled underneath.

It grows dark in the office. The sun sets. No one comes.

Someone will come for you. Thinking these words, whispering them helps me believe that they will come true.

In my mind, I wander along the streets I walked with Mrs. Rechtman. Streets that could take me home to Mama and Papa. I can picture every twist and turn. If only I could spend one more night with my parents. I realize that I may have to spend the night here, alone, under a small desk, in a dark office in an empty building.

I wonder about the other children. There must be other children who have left the ghetto with new names. But only the guards go in and out of the ghetto, not regular people. Those who are out, stay out. And those who are in can't leave.

Except Jolanta. She brings us food and clothes and medicine, she leaves and comes back again. Almost every day. *Could Jolanta have another name, like me?*

The wind rubs against the windows and the building creaks and cracks. There is no sound of another person anywhere.

I used to cry. Before the war, I cried about any little thing. If my cousin Jakub teased me, I ran to my mother, eyes full of tears. If I woke at night to the sound of a dog barking in a neighbor's yard, I rushed to my parents' room, terrified. I stopped crying the night the first bombs fell on Warsaw. Papa and Uncle Aleksander had left to fight, to defend Poland. I huddled in the basement with Mama, Grandma, Aunt Roza and Jakub. Fire fell from the sky, buildings flew up in the air and the earth roared like it was being ripped to pieces.

When the sun came up, the streets were on fire. People got busy stocking food, pulling the dead into the courtyards, putting out fires and searching for a safe place to hide for the next round of bombs. I shake my head to wipe away the memories of Warsaw on fire and take a breath to clear the crying feeling out of my chest.

I still get tightness in my chest and a tickle in my throat at a crying time. But the crying feeling never reaches my eyes, never makes tears. Even today, when Mama and Papa couldn't hold back tears, I didn't, couldn't, cry. I take another deep breath. *I'm not going to cry.* I take one of the pieces of bread from my pocket, whisper a blessing and nibble slowly. *Someone will be here before I finish this bread.*

It's such a small piece of bread, about half the size of my hand. Still, I'm determined to eat slowly. I count each bite, trying to make the bread last until I've reached one hundred. I manage eighty-seven bites, eating every crumb.

It's so late. *I won't sleep.* I try to get comfortable in the dark office, leaning against the desk.

Someone will come. I won't sleep. I close my eyes and wait.

Chapter 9

Someone is shaking my shoulders. "What is your name?"

"Anna, Anna Karwolska."

The lady looks like a teenage girl. She has straight light-brown hair and large green eyes. She takes my hands and helps me stand. We walk out of the office and down the empty hallway. There aren't any people in the large main room and our footsteps echo on the floor. We hold hands as we walk outside.

Everything is the same, but different. I look back at the door and realize that it's not the one that I entered yesterday. The building has two large doors—one leading to the ghetto and one going to the outside world. I'm out of the ghetto for the first time in over two years.

As the sun tries to come up, the girl leads the way through streets that twist and turn near the ghetto wall. Just on the other side are Mama, Papa, Mrs. Rechtman, Sonia, Halina and all of the others from the youth circle. These streets aren't full of people. There isn't anyone sleeping on the sidewalk, not a single child begging for food. I have to skip and run a bit to keep up with the girl. She's still got hold of my hand. We finally stop near the cemetery, on a bridge overlooking a giant rubbish pile.

"We have to get closer," she says, and drops my hand.

I follow her across the bridge and along a dirt path to the rubbish pile. The girl crouches behind the mound of trash and crumbled bricks and motions for me to do the same. I come closer, get down and wait beside her. A few moments ago, standing on the bridge, I was hungry. I'm always hungry. But next to all of this filthy rubbish, I can barely breathe. The smell is worse than the community bathroom, worse than the pile of manure behind the stables. The air is rotten. Every breath I take burns my nose and throat.

Just when I'm about to ask what we are doing, hoof beats approach quickly. The girl puts a hand over my head and we both curl into tight balls on the ground. It sounds as if the horse stops on the other side of the mountain of rubbish. It trots away in a matter of moments.

The girl presses her arm tight over me until we can't hear the horse at all. Then she rises slowly.

I stand and follow her to the other side of the huge rubbish pile. She bends down and digs into the grime with her bare hands. Underneath the stones and broken bricks is a wooden crate. It's a bit smaller than a doctor's bag. The girl lifts the box and, for the first time, I see her smile.

"Follow me," she says. "But stay behind me like we aren't walking together. If anyone stops me, keep walking. Walk right past me for at least two blocks, then stop at the first bench you see and wait."

I nod. It feels like years since I've had a normal conversation. The only time anyone speaks to me is to give me orders. I follow the girl and wonder about the box. *It must be full of food. What else is worth digging through disgusting trash to get?* We walk on. In time the buildings become farther apart and we turn away from the city. My legs are heavy as if my shoes are really galoshes filled with water. I put one foot in front of the other again and again.

The girl turns and waves me forward. "You can walk with me now." The wooden box is scraping her skin with every step, the insides of her elbows are bleeding.

"I can hold it," I tell her.

She shakes her head. "It will ruin your clothes."

27

"I have long sleeves and you're hurt." I hold my arms out. She surprises me and sets the box carefully in my arms.

"Please, be very careful." I match her pace and keep the box close to my chest. We're surrounded by fields now, with only a few small houses standing back from the road.

The box is heavier than a loaf of bread, heavier than twenty loaves of bread, but it is too small for that much food.

"Where are we going?"

"Straight."

"What's your name?"

"You can call me Miss."

"Miss? But, you're so young. I bet you're still a teenager."

The girl, Miss, rubs the insides of her arms. She bends and straightens her elbows. She doesn't tell me her real name. A thin man on a bike passes us. He doesn't say hello. We don't even look at him.

"We should hurry," says the girl, Miss. She speeds up and is quickly ahead of me. I focus on each step. To catch up with Miss I would have to run. Impossible. Walking is enough of a challenge.

I can do this. I lift my legs high, but they seem to come down in the same place. The grass bends and sways in the fields beside me, making my head spin. I can't keep my knees straight. I set the box on the ground, carefully. Then I collapse beside it.

Above me, Miss says, "We didn't come this far to stop here. It's the next house." The words are far away, like part of a bird's song.

I'm flying in the air. No, I'm moving forward. I'm on a horse.

I wake up when I feel myself sliding. Miss is carrying me on her back. She's bent over, setting the box next to the door of a farmhouse. She helps me slide off her back and onto my feet.

"Let's get in before we are seen," she says. Miss shifts her gaze to the box and picks it up. "Or heard," she adds.

It is cool and dark inside the farmhouse. There is a small

square table covered with a white cloth, and in the very center is a bowl full of apples. Miss sets the wooden box on a chair and tries to open it. After pulling and prying with her hands, she leaves and comes back with a tool like a short silver stick.

Miss turns the box this way and that, inspecting it. She puts the tool between the boards very carefully, as if she were making a box instead of trying to break one open. My eyes keep drifting to the bowl of apples. I haven't seen fresh fruit in over a year. *Apples. A whole bowl full of apples!* I try to remember the last time I bit into an apple. My head begins to spin again.

Miss tilts the tool and cracks one of the boards. Carefully, she moves on to the next. After four boards are pulled aside, Miss reaches her hands into the box and pulls out a tiny baby.

"What?"

"Her name is Rachel," says Miss. "You helped save her."

Chapter 10

Miss cleans Rachel and wraps her in a new blanket. Rachel doesn't squirm; she doesn't make a sound.

"Is she ill? She's so quiet."

"Induced sleep," says Miss. I don't understand what that means. "She'll wake in about half an hour."

I can't concentrate on Miss with the apples so near. *A whole bowl full of apples. Food, sitting untouched, waiting to be eaten.* I know it's impolite to ask for food. Instead, I say, "Miss, wherever did you find so many apples?"

"We have an apple tree." Then, as if she can read my mind, she takes the bowl of apples and places it in a high cupboard. Miss pours a glass of water and sets it in front of me on the table. "Broth and bread for you today. Mother insists on two days of broth and bread before any other food. You'll become terribly sick otherwise. I've seen it happen."

I drink the water and finish the bread in my pocket as Miss prepares the hot broth. When she sets it in front of me, the broth smells so strong, as if it holds the flavor of one hundred bowls of soup.

As I reach the bottom of my bowl, there is screaming and howling outside. Miss peers through the window. "It's Mother," she says. She flings the door open and runs to help. A woman marches to the house. Each of her hands holds the arm of a child. A boy and girl scream with all their might on either side of her. They have tattered clothes and dirty faces and are so thin, like skin on bones.

Miss runs behind her mother, drapes an arm around each child's shoulders and follows them into the house. Once inside, the two children fall to the floor and cry. The woman says, "We made it home." She lets out a long sigh and smiles. It is a real, true, happy smile. It makes her eyes shine and her whole face light up.

My stomach flip-flops. I haven't seen so many smiles in one day since before the war. I walk close to Miss's mother. She strokes my chin with a finger. "And who do we have here?"

"I'm Anna, ma'am."

"Yes, you are." She smiles again. "Have you had some broth? Some bread?"

"Yes, Mother," Miss answers for me. "But she really wants an apple."

The boy and girl continue to sob in the corner. The boy simply cries, but the girl calls out for her mother, as if her mama is close enough to hear her.

Miss's mother reaches for the bowl of apples. "You can't have one today," she says. "But pick the one you like and I will save it just for you."

I pick a big red apple from the top and she crinkles brown paper around it.

The boy has his arm around his little sister. She calls out, "Mama, Mama, Mama."

It makes my heart ache for Mama and Papa. I sit down next to them. "You don't have to cry," I tell them. "Everyone is nice here. There's food, broth and bread, even apples."

The boy quiets down, but the girl lets out a long howl, "Maaaaamaaaa!"

"Your mother is certainly happy you are here." I try to comfort her. But this only makes the girl cry louder.

"Our mother is dead," says the boy. "Died this morning."

I remember that I am Anna Karwolska. "My mother is dead too. So is my father. My name is Anna, what's yours?"

"Hot broth. Warm bread. Anyone hungry?" Miss sets two steaming bowls on the table.

The boy stands up first. His sister stops crying and follows him. They climb onto their chairs and drink their broth. While they are quietly eating their bread, a new cry fills the air—baby Rachel. Her voice is soft and pouty; she sounds like a small animal. Miss and her mother both rush over to hold her. Miss is first. She swoops Rachel into her arms and begins to sing. Rachel coos and stretches happily.

Miss's mother stands next to me. "You did a good job comforting those two," she tells me. "Now let's get you cleaned up." She walks out of the room.

I follow and start to tell her that I washed just yesterday, but the words stick in my mouth because in front of me is a bright white bathtub. *A bathtub!* And when she turns the knob, water runs out of the faucet. She pulls a basket off a shelf and sets it next to the tub. I lift the cloth on top to find two bars of soap, a packet of hair soap and a brush for my nails. The water runs on and on, covering the bottom of the tub and starting to fill it. I want to turn it off, save some for later. It feels like so much water to use for cleaning one person.

"What's your name?" I ask her.

She smiles and says, "You can call me Auntie."

After my bath, Auntie combs out my hair and plaits it into two braids again. When she gets to the bottom of the first braid, I hand her a strip of faded pink cloth. "Can you please fasten it off with this?"

She holds out her hand and takes the cloth without question. She does the same for the second braid too.

Chapter 11

The boy and girl who came yesterday are called Martin and Frieda. I wonder if those are their real names. Auntie's house is like a school. I soon discover that I haven't learned everything about Anna Karwolska. I have a special saint and saint's day, July 26.

"This day is as important as your birthday," Auntie tells me. "Don't forget it."

Anna Karwolska has special prayers for certain times of the day, like me. The words to the prayers are different. I learn how to bless my food saying the new prayers in Polish and in German, and how to make a cross from my head to my heart.

Frieda easily learns the prayers and has an angelic voice.

Martin complains that the lessons are too hard. I try to make a game to help him learn the prayers line by line, but he can't sit still.

When Auntie has her attention on Frieda, I follow Martin and make up a clapping game to teach him the new prayers. We move from room to room until he finds a favorite place, under the kitchen table. He learns the prayers eventually, but gets mixed up making the cross.

"Follow me," I say, pushing away a chair to make a path. He does. We practice crossing ourselves while looking in the mirror by the front door.

Miss keeps Rachel in her arms all day. She paces room to

room, looking out every window, and only sets the baby down to clean her or to wrap her in a new blanket.

"Is she sick?" I ask.

"No, she's healthy as can be."

Auntie brings three bowls of broth to the table. Martin, Frieda and I say our new prayer perfectly. The broth is just as good as yesterday. One bowl and a single piece of bread fill me as if I've just eaten a feast. Frieda and Martin lick their bowls clean.

As soon as we finish eating a bell rings outside, three loud chirps. Martin crouches under the table. Frieda and I hide behind our chairs. The sound of the bell is frightening, yet familiar.

"Children, don't be alarmed," says Auntie. "Three rings. Safe."

Auntie opens the door wide. An old lady on a bike is at the front door. A bike bell! I had one on my first bike, years ago. The woman is wearing a long black dress, black boots and a straw farmer's hat. On the back of her bike sits a large basket. She steps inside. When she takes off her hat, long gray hair falls down past her shoulders. She rubs her hands together. "Bring me the infant."

Miss sets Rachel down on the counter. The old lady unbundles Rachel and examines her the way a doctor would. Then she unrolls her sleeve and removes a piece of paper. She unfolds the paper carefully, dips her smallest finger against it and rubs her finger on Rachel's bottom lip.

I creep closer. The old lady taps the end of her finger in some powder on the paper and brushes it against Rachel's lip again and again. Rachel's eyes begin to close. The old lady dips her finger into the powder once more and pops it into Rachel's mouth. Rachel is soon fast asleep.

The woman nods, carefully folds the paper and tucks it back into her sleeve. She wraps Rachel in a blanket and takes her outside. I stand in the doorway as she snuggles little Rachel into the bottom of her basket. She covers her with another blanket and nestles about twenty eggs on top. The woman wraps her hair up and tucks it under her hat. Then she climbs onto her bicycle and rides off without a word.

The old woman rides off along the same path that I carried Rachel yesterday. I feel a tug at my heart, like I'm being pulled out of Mama's arms, like Papa's hands are slipping away from mine. "No. Stop." I step away from the house. One step. Two steps. Three steps. And I'm off, running to catch the bike, running to Rachel.

Miss's arms surround me. She nearly lifts me into the air. "Anna." Her voice is an astonished whisper. "What are you thinking? You couldn't even walk that distance yesterday without collapsing. And today you're fit to run?" She releases me and I fall to the ground, sitting on the dirt path. She stands beside me. I watch until the woman and her bicycle become a small speck, then disappear. *Good-bye, Rachel.*

Miss holds out her hand. I take it and she pulls me up. "You must never leave the house, Anna. It is too dangerous."

Suddenly I want to cry. I want to kick and scream and shout. My feet fall in step next to Miss. But I can't stop my thoughts from pouring out of my mouth. "I helped save her. And now she's gone."

Miss nods. We approach the side door. Auntie's hand is on the knob, ready to shut the door behind us. Her face is full of sympathy. She lifts her arms up as if she's going to hug me, but I march past her. My sadness has grown so big it's turned into anger.

When Auntie and Miss unroll our bed mat at the end of the day, my head is full of new songs and prayers. I worked so hard to remember them all day, but now, at night, I want them out of my mind. Being another person isn't just about remembering. It's about forgetting. I don't want to forget being Anna Bauman.

Martin and Frieda cry for a few minutes and then fall fast

asleep. I listen to Auntie and Miss through the open bedroom door. I hear Auntie call Miss "Alicia."

I will keep calling her Miss, but I tuck the name inside my heart like a secret.

As I'm about to fall asleep, I hear Auntie say "The brother and sister leave tomorrow."

"What about Anna?" Miss asks.

I think I hear her say "A day or two more." But I'm so sleepy, I can't be sure.

Chapter 12

We wake to find three bowls of broth and three apples on the table. My apple is still wrapped in brown paper. I peel back the paper and hold it up to my nose. The apple smells so perfect and fresh. It smells too good to eat.

I set the apple by my bowl. Knowing that it's so close and all mine makes me feel like singing one of the songs I learned yesterday.

Martin's had a few bites, but Frieda is looking at me expectantly. Instantly, I remember the new prayers. "Martin, stop eating. We must bless our food." We recite the prayer, remembering to make the cross before and after just as we were taught. I look up at Auntie and her eyes are smiling.

My broth is even better than yesterday. With the apple on my mind and the smell in my nose, the broth tastes like apple soup. Martin and Frieda start on their apples first. Watching them eat makes me think of baby Rachel. Someday, when she's big enough, she will eat apples. As soon as I finish my broth, I wrap my hands around my apple. I close my eyes. It smells more powerful than just one apple. I think I can smell the bark and the branches—maybe even hear the leaves of the apple tree rustling in the wind. My apple smells like the outside, like the whole free world.

I am in two places at once. My body is in Auntie's house holding an apple in my hands. But my mind is climbing the big apple tree at the park across from my home. The memories flood into my head the way sunlight pours into a room when the curtains are pulled back. I was six years old the first time I scrambled into that tree. It was the first day of school. Half of me wanted to climb high, to the very top. The rest of me was afraid of falling. Grandma's warning rang in my ears: *Don't climb too high and you won't have to fall.* I sat on a sturdy bottom branch and feasted on apples. A voice brings my thoughts back to Auntie's house.

"Aren't you going to try a bite?" Miss asks.

I have to blink a few times to see the apple clearly. I'm holding it in both my hands above the empty bowl. Miss, Auntie, Martin and Frieda are all looking at me.

"Of course I am!" I open my mouth and pause for a moment. I say the blessing quickly in my mind: *Blessed are you, Lord our God, King of the universe, who creates fruit from the tree.* Their eyes are all on me as I take a big bite. The apple is crisp and juicy. It tastes even better than I'd imagined.

After breakfast, Miss whisks Martin and Frieda off to have their baths and to mend their clothes. Auntie sits down next to me and begins our lessons. I learn about holidays and church. Auntie asks me the same questions over and over again. Then she asks the most difficult question of all. "Tell me about your parents," she says.

At first I think she means my real parents. "My parents?"

"Yes. How did they die?"

That's when I realize she is asking about Anna Karwolska's parents. I chew on my bottom lip. This is a strange new feeling. Obviously Auntie knows everything. She knows where I came from. Otherwise why bother to teach me all of the new things? But Auntie and Miss are the same. They never say *We want to see how well you can pretend to be the new Anna.*

"How did they die?" Auntie asks again.

"The war," I manage to say. "They were killed in the war. Squished."

"Squished?" asks Auntie. "Like under a building?"

"Yes, the building was bombed." I remember a family whose house was bombed. They were sitting against a wall in the basement. When the bomb fell on the house, half of a wall collapsed. The mother and son survived. The father and two daughters died instantly. "I was sitting right next to my mother when it happened. The wall toppled on my parents, but not on me."

Auntie folds her arms around me and sways with me from side to side. I wonder why Auntie is comforting me. *Because I pretended so well? Or does she think what I said about my parents is true?*

I bite my tongue until it hurts. I stop myself from blurting out *It's not true. I'm Anna Bauman. My parents are alive in Warsaw, in the ghetto.*

I expected pretending to get easier. But instead my secrets grow bigger every day. Now they seem so big that they might burst out of me.

Chapter 13

Martin and Frieda sit at the table. They do not look like the same two screaming children I first saw two days ago. They aren't pale and frightened. They are calm. They are clean. And they are talking. "What's this?" Frieda asks her brother, pointing to her plate.

Martin looks at Auntie.

"It's cheese," Auntie says.

"Cheese," repeats Martin.

"Have I eaten it before? Do I like it?" Frieda asks.

Martin looks a bit uncertain. He nods. "You had it once. You loved it. You asked for cheese all the time. Don't you remember?"

Frieda tries it. And she likes it.

Before the table is cleared, a horse and cart stops in back of the house. Auntie rushes off to talk with the driver. Miss gathers Martin and Frieda in her arms. "It's time. Remember everything we talked about."

Martin takes his sister's hand and walks with her to the back door. In the doorway, he stops and turns to me. "So long," he says.

The driver is at the back of the cart waiting. He lifts Frieda up first, then Martin. Next he shakes out a dark blue blanket. The blanket covers Martin and Frieda, just as the blanket on the old lady's bicycle covered Rachel.

My head is exploding with questions. My stomach is full

of thunder. I watch the horse and cart drive away. Miss stands close as if she's afraid I'll run after them like I ran after Rachel. The cart shrinks in the distance. When I can't see it anymore, I walk to where Auntie is sitting at the table.

"Auntie, can I still remember my old songs? My own prayers?"

"You may remember them, Anna. But you mustn't speak them. Not to anyone. Not until after the war."

"I won't. I promise." Auntie sounds like Papa, always talking about after the war, always believing that the war will really end. "I like the new songs. I even like the prayers. But which one, which religion, is right?"

"Right? What do you mean *right*?"

"Which religion is right . . . about God?"

Auntie brushes both of my braids off my shoulders and looks straight into my eyes. "This is what I know," she says. "I know it is *right* that the world has *both* religions."

x

Chapter 14

I lie awake a long time. Rachel is gone. Martin and Frieda are gone. Tomorrow I will be gone too, sleeping in another place, away from Auntie and Miss. Just thinking about it makes me feel alone.

I concentrate on each room in Auntie's house. In this bedroom I could hide in the closet, curled into a ball. In the kitchen I can slide behind the large chest that holds Auntie's dishes, my back flat against the wall. The bathroom has no hiding place, but there's a low window for escape.

I'm growing sleepy, but I toss and turn because I can't imagine tomorrow. I bring up memories of the past. I know what to expect there. My mind has been buzzing with every new detail about being Anna Karwolska. It crowds out my memories of Anna Bauman. I don't want to forget. I make a promise to myself: *I won't forget.*

I imagine every holiday with Mama and Papa, each room of my old house. I think about my grandfather's voice, strong and rumbly, as he prayed. I can see each photograph framed on my grandmother's mantel. Tonight the memories don't make me sad. They don't even make me feel homesick. Instead, I feel rich. Every memory, every word is a part of me.

I hear Grandma's voice in her special language: *You can't grow corn on the ceiling. If you can't do as you wish, do what you can.* When I asked her if she wished she could play the piano like Mama or act onstage like Uncle Aleksander, she said, "If I would be like someone else, who will be like me?"

If I'm becoming Anna Karwolska, who will be Anna Bauman?

I must be both. Anna Karwolska all day and whenever anyone is near. And Anna Bauman at night, when I'm alone.

In the morning, the same horse and cart stops behind the house. I know it's my turn to say good-bye. When I hug Miss, a lump grows in my chest. I mean to say "I'll never forget you." But instead, "Don't ever forget me" comes out of my mouth. I don't try to correct it, because as soon as I hear the words I know they are truer than true.

"Never," says Miss, hugging me tightly. She places an apple in my hand. Auntie kisses my cheeks three times and presents me with another apple.

With an apple in each pocket, I walk to the cart. The man scoops me up. He tells me to be still and covers me with a blanket. In less than a minute there is a tug and a bump and the cart is moving, taking me away.

Chapter 15

I wonder if I will be taken to the same place as Martin and Frieda. I'm in the same cart, under the same blanket, being pulled by the same horse and driven by the same driver. I curl my arm under my head to keep it from hitting against the bottom of the cart with every bump. I count the nights away from Mama and Papa. I spent one night alone under a desk and three nights with Miss and Auntie. Only four nights, yet everything is different. I wonder what Mama and Papa are doing right this very moment. Are they inside the small room? Out on the streets? Do they have enough food?

Stop it! It's daytime. You are Anna Karwolska.

I wish I could imagine my next home. Every time I try, Auntie's farmhouse comes up. I wonder if I will be with another mother and daughter. Maybe I will study more. Maybe I will actually go to a real school.

I practice answering questions in case we are stopped by soldiers or police. I will be able to say my name, my birthday and saint's day, talk about my parents. I can even talk about holiday decorations and say prayers.

What if someone asks *Why are you hiding under a blanket?* For that question, I have no answer.

Here in the dark, I feel like I'm being watched. The man driving might be turning around to check on me. Someone may pass by us and peer into the cart. I must keep perfectly still. Each time the cart stops, I think we've arrived—or we're being stopped by soldiers. My heart leaps into my throat and pounds like a giant drum. I take a deep breath, force my heart back into my chest and feel the strong tug of the cart moving forward again.

It's cool outside but hot under the thick blanket. My hair sticks to my forehead. My throat is so dry it hurts to swallow. My stomach rumbles. Eating three times a day has taught it to be hungry more often. I feel for the apples in my pockets. My stomach is only complaining. I'm not hungry, not really.

I practice everything Auntie and Miss taught me. When I get to the end, I start from the beginning again. Over and over I say each prayer and sing every song in my head at least ten times.

Finally the horse stops for a long time. The man pulls the blanket from me. He holds out his hands and says, "Down we go."

I leap from the cart. When my feet hit the ground I feel the shock all the way up to my knees. We're surrounded by forest except for a giant white wall. It's so tall and so long, I don't realize at first that it is part of a building. The building is large, bigger than a hospital. The man marches ahead and I follow. As we get closer to the wall, I see that is connected to a tall, beautiful church.

The man stops by a wooden door. "Please, not a sound while we are inside. And act your very best," he says. His voice is thin and sounds a bit nervous. He knocks and a woman's voice calls out. We enter an office with dark furniture. A woman in a brown smock and white hat sits behind a desk covered with papers.

"Sister Maria," says the man. "I've brought you Anna. All of her papers are in order. Here is her birth certificate, her baptismal certificate, and she has a valid ration card for food."

Sister Maria stands but ignores the man. Instead, she speaks to me. "The other children are eating at the end of the hall. There isn't food to spare. But there's enough. Please join them."

"Thank you." I leave the room and turn in the direction Sister Maria pointed.

Before I take three steps, I hear Sister Maria say, "I told you last time we have no room. The children are lined up ear to ear with hungry bellies. What am I to do?"

"I brought food," the man says. "A great deal of food. Have pity, Sister. There are so many children. We depend on you." I hurry down the hall. I don't want anyone to think I am listening to their conversation on purpose.

Statues line the hallway, giant men and woman in colorful clothes with golden circles over their heads. The statues don't look across the hall at each other, they all look down. As I walk, it feels like their eyes follow my every step. A huge statue faces me at the end of the hall. It is a woman with a kind and caring face, a face like Auntie's. A chubby child clasps his arms around her neck but the woman holds both of her arms out, as if wanting to welcome a lost friend into a tender hug. For a moment I forget my hunger. I even forget that I'm in a strange new place. I look up at the woman and wish I could fly up to that statue and let myself be wrapped in those loving arms.

Two large wooden doors stand on either side of the statue. I'm not sure if I should open the door on the left or the door on the right. I look back at the statue. The woman is smiling at me. Her face seems to say *Everything will be all right. Don't be afraid.*

I open the door on the left. Both doors open to the same large room, a room full of tables and children, girls of all ages. For just a moment, one hundred pairs of eyes look my way. Then the girls turn back to their food and begin eating again. A tall woman places a hand on my shoulder. She leads me to a seat and brings me a bowl of soup.

The soup tastes like warm water and cooked carrots. There is also dark bread. I drink every drop of soup and eat every crumb of bread. Just as Sister Maria said, there is none to spare. But there is enough.

Chapter 16

A lady with fair skin and blue eyes sits opposite me. She has blond hair just past her shoulders. "I'm Monika," she says. "I'm the oldest girl here." She nearly smiles.

"Oh, I thought you were a teacher."

Monika gives me a puzzled look. "It's just us girls and the sisters, the nuns." I nod my head as if I know what she's talking about.

Another girl sits next to Monika. She has short brown hair and wears a scowl. She doesn't introduce herself, but begins to question me. She asks my name, my birthday and where I came from. I tell her Anna Karwolska's hometown.

"That's far away. You must have family near here."

I shake my head. I've never thought about Anna Karwolska's aunts and uncles and cousins.

"Well, who brought you here, then?" The girl's scowl grows deeper.

"I—I—"

"Let her be, Klara," Monika interrupts. "Show some kindness."

"I'm going to be a nun one day," Klara announces. "I'm going to be in charge here."

Later that evening, when it's time for bed, I follow Monika into a large room with draped curtains. There are two rows of beds with a small table beside each one.

Klara blocks my way. "You're with the little girls," she says. "You have to be at least nine to sleep in this room."

"But I am nine," I say.

"Liar." Klara crosses her arms. "Did you forget you told me your birthday?"

I am nine. But Anna Karwolska is eight and will be for a few more months. How could I remember my birthday but forget my age? "I mean eight," I mumble. "I thought you said eight."

"Come, I'll take you," says Monika. I expect her to glare at Klara, but she doesn't. Perhaps Monika never scowls. She takes me across the hall to a room crowded with cribs and cots. Monika wanders along the row of beds, finally stopping to smile down at a little girl. "Eva, I've brought you a new friend."

Eva gets up on her knees and bounces on the bed.

"She's four," Monika says. "I'm sure the two of you will get along nicely."

I climb into bed next to Eva.

"What's your name?" she asks. I tell her. "What's your job?"

"I don't have a job here, yet. What's yours?"

"Make sure the babies don't cry. Clean the babies that the sisters tell me to clean. Leave the other babies alone. Never disturb a sleeping baby. Stay in my place. Do as I'm told." She nods, satisfied. "And keep silent."

Eva snuggles right up next to me, as though she's known me her whole life, and closes her eyes. *I'm lucky to be with the little ones. I don't like to sleep alone. Besides, I have nothing to put on a table.*

Soon the babies and small children stop crying. Eva's breathing grows even and slow and I know she's asleep too. I stare at the slightly open door where a sliver of light enters the room. I've tried to be Anna Karwolska all day. I practiced in my head in the cart. I'm working so hard, but still Klara almost caught me.

I'm eight. I'm eight. I'm eight. I'm eight, I chant inside my head. *How could I forget something so simple? What would they have done? Would they send me away? Turn me over to the Germans?*

Everyone here is Catholic. They know the prayers, the holidays, the songs. They know how to behave. Everyone in this whole building is exactly the same, has been exactly the same since the moment they were born. Everyone except me.

I must try with all my might to be Anna Karwolska. I should practice more. But I can't. It's like carrying something heavy a great distance. I have to set it down and rub my arms and catch my breath. Just for a few minutes before I sleep I have to put Anna Karwolska out of my mind. I can't forget Anna Bauman.

I close my eyes and slip back in time. I remember every flower in the garden in my backyard, the smell of my grandmother's house, sawdust swirling out the door of Papa's shop, the wedding of my aunt. My first home and my big family feel so far away. I remember Papa's finger tracing around mine against the small cool window in the ghetto. And the poem:

The bright flame of truth pursue,
Seek to discover new ways.
Secrets will be revealed to you,
Your soul grows and becomes new.

I must not forget being Anna Bauman. Remembering my real self is a bright flame of truth inside me.

Chapter 17

A bell ringing outside our door wakes us. The sisters bustle in to take care of the babies. The little girls get up and dressed. They line up by the door in stocking feet. I'm the only one lucky enough to have shoes.

I stand in line with the other girls to get my morning bread. When they cross themselves, I cross myself. When they say a blessing, I mumble along. The blessings are almost the same as the ones Auntie taught me.

After breakfast we go to prayer service. When Klara passes me she leans close to my ear and whispers, "Liar." I jump. For a moment I think she knows I'm Anna Bauman, knows I'm Jewish. But then I realize I earned the nickname Liar last night when I said I was nine.

I copy the other girls during prayer service as they sit, stand and kneel. Sister Maria's voice is strong and booming, like a man's, when she reads from the Bible. Though when she sings, her voice is light and climbs high.

At lunch Klara walks near me twice, leaning in close to whisper in my ear. I keep my expression blank and look down at my food.

After lunch some children file out to go to lessons. I stare after them. *I want to go to school.* The tall nun who steered me to a seat yesterday places a hand on my shoulder. She leads me into the kitchen.

The kitchen! Certainly I have the best work assignment in the whole place.

She places a broom in my hand and waves her arm. "When the two of you are finished here, the dining room is next." I'm assigned to sweep along with a girl named Roza.

"The nuns are eating now." Roza nods to a door at our left and takes a deep breath. "It smells so delicious."

I smell nothing except a kitchen so damp it is as if some of the outside has crept in. Ignoring Roza, I begin to sweep. She walks beside me, dragging her broom behind her. "Watch out for treasures."

"Treasures?" I keep sweeping.

"There! You have one!" She pounces on the pile of dirt in front of my broom and pulls out a strip of paper. "Potato peel," she says, and pops it into her mouth.

I wonder if it really was a potato peel. And if there will be more treasures. A few moments later Roza bends down and takes something white from her dirt pile. Without inspecting it first, she eats it. "Eggshell," she says. "Very nutritious." And I know she has the hunger. I saw many people hungry like Roza in the ghetto. Hungry deep into their bones. So hungry, the hunger infected their minds.

I sweep the kitchen and the dining room. Roza follows along, inspecting each of my piles and sweeping the dirt into a dustpan.

"What now?" I ask.

"Finished!" Roza lifts her broom high and walks quickly back to the kitchen. She tucks the broom into a corner by the door. I place mine next to hers.

The door is calling me. I push it open a crack and look outside. The white wall stands strong along the courtyard. Colorful leaves carpet the ground near the church. Tall pines reach high into the sky. *I am so very far from the rest of the world. How will Mama and Papa find me way out here?*

Chapter 18

Sundays are so important, and so different, I soon stop counting the days and begin counting Sundays. Today is my tenth Sunday. Prayer service is much longer and even more serious. All of the nuns attend and one plays the organ. Sister Maria's voice is so loud, so strong, so certain. It seems as if Sister Maria has the entire Bible memorized and all of history too.

When the organ music plays, I remember Mama's hands running over the piano keys in our home. She played so beautifully, people would stop on the street outside to listen. I think Mama would like this music. I stand and sing with the other girls.

The orphanage is full—over a hundred girls and several dozen sisters. The small sounds like footsteps, talking and music covered the silence so well that it took me a few days to feel the quiet of this place. There is no begging. No shouting. No gunfire.

I wonder if Papa still stands at the window where he traced my hand, listening to children begging for bread. It seems like a long time ago.

No one here ever questions me about my name, birthday or where I'm from. I don't think about being Anna Karwolska or Anna Bauman. I'm just Anna. Until Klara whispers in my ear.

Klara doesn't have a job. She sits in the chapel for hours reading the Bible and praying. I hope it's true, what Sister Maria says about prayers filling our hearts and souls with the light of God. Maybe if she prays enough, Klara will stop whispering in my ear.

I'm not the only one Klara taunts. At least with me she only whispers. When the sisters aren't near, Klara stands in front of Roza and waves her arms. "Bird Girl. Tweet tweet, Bird Girl!" Roza ignores her. Klara laughs. "You don't understand?" She tweets and caws, following Roza around the room. *Why doesn't anyone stop her?*

After sweeping one day, Roza stands in front of a closet door. She has her face pressed to the keyhole and is breathing deeply. When she notices I'm watching her, she says, "Food." I stand beside her and try the knob. The door isn't locked. I pull it open, just a bit, only enough for us to see inside. Roza's right. It's a large pantry. The shelves are piled high with sacks of flour, jars of food, even a bit of sugar.

I close the door and smile, a real, wide smile. *We are rich with food!*

Chapter 19

One afternoon, Klara follows me and Roza as we sweep the dining room. The sisters are in their separate room, eating their lunch. Klara starts her act of waving her arms. Roza pushes past her, the broom leading the way. "Hey, Bird Girl," complains Klara. "You got dust on my socks." She jumps in front of Roza again.

Roza plows past her, pushing the broom, her head down. Klara rips the broom out of Roza's hands and pushes her. Girls file in from the hall. They see Roza stumble backward. I think at first that they will help, but they only stand near the door and watch. ,

Roza bends down for her broom. Klara shoves with both hands and Roza tumbles to the ground. I learn why Klara calls Roza Bird Girl. "Go ahead, bend down. Peck for food on the ground. We all watch you do it, Bird Girl."

The others back out the door, afraid. I try to meet their eyes but they look away.

Roza climbs slowly to her knees. As she reaches for her broom Klara kicks it away. Roza looks to me for help, about to cry.

"Stop it!" I say. "Just stop." Klara turns to face me and my voice is gone, stuck in my throat, afraid like Roza. Klara stands tall, her face red and furious. She steps toward me. I must say something. "Be kind," I say. "Please, be kind."

Klara spins around and notices the others staring at her. "Why should I be kind to a liar and a bird girl? Why should

I even speak to either of you?" She marches to the door and the other girls scatter. Klara holds her head high, marching proudly. She is so certain that she alone is right. It makes my cheeks burn. She's like the soldiers standing guard at the ghetto, so few holding in thousands.

Klara turns back to us, a superior smirk on her face. The distance between us makes me brave. "Please, don't speak to us," I call to her. "We really wish you wouldn't. No one wants to hear your ugly words and your mean voice."

The other girls' faces are frozen in shock. I turn to help Roza, but she's already on her feet, sweeping again.

Klara corners me in the hallway between the bedrooms that night. "Apologize." Every girl in the whole orphanage is watching. "Apologize for what you said to me earlier."

I open my mouth but I can't speak. Klara's hand springs out in an instant and she clutches my arm. I should apologize and get away, go hide. But I can't force an apology out of my mouth, though she's clutching my arm so tightly her nails are digging into my skin. "Certainly," I say. "I will apologize after you apologize to Roza." I turn to look for Roza, but she must be hiding behind another girl.

"You're going to regret this," says Klara. "I can tell when a girl is a liar or a cuckoo bird." She pauses and looks deep in my eyes. "I know everything." She releases my arm, turns away and slips into the room for the older girls.

I lie awake with Eva snuggled warmly against me, her breath even and slow. Having her near helps melt away the burning in my chest, the tightening of my throat. I force myself to forget about Klara. Instead I am Anna Bauman.

Running outside the door of my grandparent's house on a warm day, Jakub calling to Grandma through an open window, "We're taking Felek with us." Felek's chain hitting the ground near his feet.

Before we made it around the house, Grandma was standing at the front door. "Don't come home with a wet dog. Keep that dog out of the lake." Jakub opened the gate and Felek pushed his head against my hand begging for a scratch. "Answer me!"

"Yes," Jakub answered. And we were off running through the fields, down the country roads, Felek's bark like laughter behind us. On our way back we took the path by the lake, throwing sticks for Felek to chase. Before long Jakub and I were wadding to our knees in the lake, our feet sunk deep into the squishy bottom and Felek swimming happily around us.

Inside the gate, Jakub forgot to clip Felek to his chain. He followed us into the house, a blur of water, mud and grass.

Grandma burst out of the kitchen waving a wooden spoon in the air. "Jakub!"

Instead of confessing, he looked at me. "Anna did it," he said. "She threw a stick in the water for him to chase."

She towered over me, furious.

"No, it was Jakub. He went into the water first," I insisted.

We argued back and forth. I couldn't remember. *Did I throw the first stick into the lake?* "Silence." Grandma's voice was low, as if she was too angry to shout. Felek sat next to her feet, his tail thumping happily. "No more stories. The truth. The truth is the safest lie."

Jakub and I spoke at the same time. "It was me," we both said.

Grandma frowned at us. "I knew it. You both made this mess"—she waved her arms around the room—"and you'll both clean it up."

In the middle of the night, the morning bell rings. It's far away and growing louder. I'm still so sleepy. The bell is ringing right next to my ear. I open my eyes and see someone rush out of the dark room. A few of the babies begin to cry.

By the time I look around the room, everyone is awake. Sister Maria and Sister Danielle rush in. "What is the meaning of this, Anna?" Sister Maria's face is pale in the dark room. She holds the copper bell up for me to see.

"I don't know. I was sleeping." *How did the bell get beside my bed?*

Monika pokes her head into our room. Klara's right behind her. She flashes me a knowing smile. *Klara!*

Monika clears her throat. "Is everything all right, Sister Maria? Can I help?"

"Back to sleep," says Sister Maria. "Everyone, back to sleep."

The next day, I learn why everyone ignores Klara. Standing up to her doesn't work. In addition to sweeping with Roza, I'm assigned two new jobs: wringing the laundry with Sister Danielle and scrubbing floors of the bathrooms alone, on my hands and knees.

I dip my brush into the bucket and scrub the floor around the toilet. Dirt makes tiny circle trails in the water, following my brush. I'm not afraid of hard work, tired hands or blistered skin. But my stomach is tumbling with another fear. Klara. *What will she do next? Would the sisters send me away if they think I'm a troublemaker?*

Mama and Papa should take care of me. They shouldn't have sent me away. Klara is out to get me and there is nothing I can do about it. I wipe up the last of the water as the sun sends light through the square window, making the floor sparkle. I would wash ten floors to have a day without Klara. I would wash a hundred floors to see Mama and Papa again. How I wish they could come here where we have food and beds and no soldiers. I know it doesn't make sense, to have parents and live in an orphanage, but I would wash a thousand, even a hundred thousand floors for that wish to come true.

Eva stands by the door as I'm rinsing my bucket. "Your floor is sparkly." It isn't my floor, but I am the one who made it shine. I smile. "Hurry, Anna. Downstairs. Something good. Something very good."

I rush behind her, the bucket swinging on my arm. Everyone

is in front of the window. I look over their shoulders and see snow, large fluffy flakes, falling from the sky.

The sisters let us go outside. It doesn't matter that none of us have coats and only a few girls have shoes. I spin and twirl in the snow. Even though it snows every winter, this particular snowfall feels like a miracle.

Big flakes land and melt like sparkling jewels in the hair of the girls around me. Small beads of water from the melting snow shimmer on my arms. I am cold. And sparkling. And alive. When I hear it the first time, I almost don't recognize the sound. It escapes from Eva's mouth. She's smiling and looking up at me. She makes the sound again. Laughter. I haven't heard it in such a long, long time. I lift her in my arms and spin her around, her head back and her mouth open. She's trying to catch a snowflake on her tongue. When I set her down, she throws her arms around my waist. "That was wonderful," she says.

I smile and agree.

She motions for me to bend over so she can whisper in my ear. I bend down. Her little hands are cold against my cheek and her warm breath covers my ear. "I love you," she says.

I whisper in her ear, "I love you too."

The next morning at breakfast we hear a sound. It's a loud humming noise, like the machines in Papa's shop. Like the machine he used to cut wood.

An older girl names the sound. "A car."

Another girl corrects her. "Cars."

Chapter 20

"Stay seated," booms Sister Maria. Her arms are raised and it makes her look taller. She holds her head high and her shoulders back as she leaves the dining hall. A few other nuns follow her. The other sisters walk up and down between the tables.

The rumble of the cars grows louder and louder. It sounds so close, as if a car will burst through the wall and right into this room.

We've all finished eating now, but we don't dare rise or make a sound. We hear only Sister Maria at first. "All is in order. There's nothing of your concern."

Then other voices reach us. Loud. Strong. Demanding. Speaking German. *Soldiers!*

Suddenly my hands are icy cold and a chill travels up my arms and through my entire body. I'm much colder than I was last night, spinning in the snow with flakes falling all around. I want to run to a hiding place. *That's what Anna Bauman would do. Anna Karwolska doesn't need to hide. Anna Karwolska is Catholic, like the other girls here. She's safe.*

The soldiers storm into the room and line up on both sides. Sister Maria is nowhere to be seen. A soldier begins speaking in German. Sister Danielle translates for the girls who don't understand.

We are lined up in the front of the room by our age. My toes are curled, pushed tight against the ends of my shoes. I shift from foot to foot. The soldier in charge splits us into groups.

I'm with girls who are seven and eight in a line near the front of the room. A red-faced soldier sits at the table. He motions us forward one by one.

Sister Maria hurries into the room, her arms full of papers.

Inside my mind, I'm repeating everything Mama and Auntie taught me. I bite my lips to make sure they aren't moving. My hands are ice cold and shaking. I clasp them together to keep them still. Someone moves behind me and I have a sudden fear that it's Klara and she will announce to the soldiers that I'm a liar. I turn my head, relieved it isn't Klara but Sister Maria.

I glance to the older girls and find Klara standing next to Monika. Her hands are clasped too. Her head is bent and her lips are moving as if in prayer. I study the girls in front of me as they speak to the soldier. They nod their heads, move their hands.

I hear Grandma's voice in my mind. *With lies you will go far, but not back again.* Before the war, she shared her sayings to remind me to be good. Now I turn each word over in my mind. *With lies you will go far*—escape, be free. *But not back again.* It's true. If I'm caught they probably won't send me back to the ghetto, back to Mama and Papa. *The truth is the safest lie.* Maybe before the war, but not now, not for me. The soldiers could shoot me right here in front of everyone. The only way to see my family again is to stay alive, and to do that I must be the best liar in the world.

Most girls only talk to the soldier for a minute or two. But Veronica, a girl who sleeps two cots away from me, is questioned for a long time.

When it's my turn, I hurry to sit opposite the soldier. The faster I begin, the sooner I will finish.

"Hello, little girl." The soldier is just pretending to be nice. I can tell because his face doesn't match his words.

"Hello, sir."

"Tell me your name."

"My name is Anna."

"Your full name."

"Anna Karwolska." Just then Sister Maria steps beside the soldier and passes him some papers, my papers. She moves on to the next table.

The soldier asks the usual questions. All of the questions that I have practiced. I'm ready with my answers before he finishes asking the questions.

Then he asks a question that I've never practiced. "What type of work does your father do?"

"My father is dead, sir." I don't feel sad or afraid telling him that my father is dead. I never knew Anna Karwolska's father. Maybe it would help if I share a little bit of truth. "He made furniture." I want to catch the words as soon as they are out of my mouth. I don't know if making furniture is a job only a Jewish papa would have.

But the solider just nods his head, as if he's bored. "What type of food did you eat for Christmas dinner?"

"The very best of food."

"What type?"

"All types. There were sweets and meat and vegetables and . . ."—I swallow, thinking of all the good food—"sweets."

"What exactly?"

"I'm not sure. I was very young and it was so long ago." It's true. Anna Karwolska would have been even younger than I was before the war began.

"Anna. Anna. Anna." I don't like the way he says my name. "Have you answered every question truthfully?"

I swallow. "Yes, sir."

The soldier reaches under the table and a moment later metal clinks against the wooden tabletop. "Do you know what that is?" I do, but I can't speak. "It's my gun." He smiles.

It's a shiny silver gun with a black handle. There's a screw connecting the handle. It seems like if I had the right tool and a moment to myself, I could remove that screw and the whole gun would fall to pieces.

"It's your gun," I say.

"I will use this gun, Anna. If you've told me a lie, I will shoot you and all the other children here. Do you understand?"

The screw is a small silver circle on a black rectangle. "It's not made properly," I say, staring at the screw.

"What?"

"The gun. It's not made properly. There's a screw showing on the outside."

"Anna. This is very serious."

I know it's serious. I understand that more than any of the other girls in this room. "My papa always said that when furniture is made correctly, no one can see how the pieces are put together. But with your gun—"

He laughs. "Anna, you really are the daughter of a carpenter."

He takes his gun off the table and for a moment I think it means I'm caught.

But he looks past me and says, "Next." So I scramble out of my chair and stand with the others who have already been questioned. We stand waiting for them to finish and leave us alone. But when they've questioned each girl, they don't leave. The sisters cook an early lunch and serve it to the soldiers. We watch them eat what would have been our lunch.

They talk and laugh and eat. I can't stop thinking about the soldier who questioned me and how easily he brought out his gun. Every soldier eating in this room has a gun. When they finish their meal, the one in charge gives his men an order. He says to gather the food. *But they have just finished eating their food.*

The soldiers go into the kitchen. And I know they will find the pantry. A minute later they march past us, each one with full arms. Some have a sack of grain on their shoulder, some have two. Others carry jars of vegetables or armloads of cabbages. Then they circle back empty-handed for more. We watch silently as they haul away every last bit of our food. There is crashing in the kitchen as if they are smashing everything to bits.

Sometime amid the chaos, Eva has found her way to me. She reaches up for my hand. When the engines start up again, we don't move. After the sounds of the cars fade, Sister Maria speaks. "Girls, bow your heads. We will pray."

We do as we are told and Sister Maria recites four prayers. I open my eyes, just a bit, and see her looking at the ceiling. She raises her voice and continues to pray. I don't know these words. I don't even understand the language.

All of us are openly looking at Sister Maria now. Her head is tilted up to the heavens. Her hands are at her chest.

"What is she saying?" Eva whispers to me.

"It's Latin," a girl beside me answers. "She's talking directly to God."

I can feel her words, even though I don't understand them. It sounds the same in any language. Sister Maria is begging.

Chapter 21

We wake with rumbling, impatient bellies. The little ones woke up often last night. Outside the windows is a thick blanket of snow. The snow is so white that it makes the world seem brighter. We file down to breakfast as always but the smell of baking bread is missing.

Instead of lining up for food, we simply sit in our usual places and wait.

Sister Maria stands in front of the room. She leads us in prayer. I'm surprised that her voice is so kind. We give thanks for our safety, for our home, for the abundance of the world around us. She offers us a bit of praise by giving thanks that we are helpful and caring for one another. Finally she thanks God for his love and attention. We slowly leave the dining room for morning service, as though the prayer was our breakfast instead of food.

After morning service, Sister Danielle steers me and Monika to the kitchen. The tall table where the vegetables were chopped is destroyed. It is just a stack of broken wood by the door. The basin under the sink is cracked and the water faucet has been ripped away from the pipe.

Sister Maria is discussing how to fix the faucet with another nun. Sister Danielle hands me and Monika each a large bowl. "Fill it up with snow. Clean snow." Perhaps Sister Danielle chose us because we both have shoes.

It's cold but there's not a bit of wind in the courtyard. The snow seeps into my worn shoes; my feet are wet in three steps. I scoop up the clean snow with my bare hands, packing it into the bowl to get as much as possible.

When it's full, I bring my bowl inside to Sister Danielle, who pours it into a pot. "Hurry, get more," she says, passing me the empty bowl.

Monika and I scoop snow into our bowls as fast as we can. In time, Sister Danielle has two pots of melting snow. She lights the fire under each pot, giving thanks that our burners weren't destroyed.

"Keep an eye on that snow as it melts," she says, and slips out the back door.

Sister Maria is laying out tools by the sink. "It was made by man. It can be repaired by man."

I watch the snow shrink into the pot as it melts from the bottom. I'm certain we will be drinking melted snow for lunch.

When Sister Danielle returns, she stands between us and hands each of us a potato peeler. "Do you know how to use these?" We nod. "Today, I want you to use it in a different way. Instead of removing the peel and throwing it away, I want you to peel the vegetable into tiny pieces and add it to the boiling water." Vegetable. She said vegetable. We have food.

She hands us each a carrot. My carrot is thin. It's also freezing and wet because Sister Danielle just scrubbed it clean with snow. She watches us shave our carrots, instructing us to make thinner strips. "Get as much from that carrot as you can."

The boiling water warms my hands as I peel the carrot into the pot. Slowly. Slowly. Bit by bit. When my carrot is just a sliver, too small to peel, I turn it over in my hands. I want to put it in my mouth. Instead, I open my hand so it falls into the soup.

I glance to my left; Monika's finished too. Sister Danielle nods at us. "You now know my recipe for one-carrot soup."

That night after Eva drifts off to sleep, I become Anna Bauman again. I try to remember my old home without thinking of food. I focus my attention on my family. But I can't help but picture Mama peeling vegetables, Aunt Roza cutting fruits, Grandfather blessing our meals, Papa slicing warm bread. Even my cousin Jakub, who has probably never helped prepare a meal in his life, reminds me of food. I picture Jakub standing next to a pile of apples, blowing the hair out of his eyes and throwing an apple so it splats against the side of Papa's shop. He threw over a dozen before Mama and Aunt Roza caught on and made him clean up his mess.

Chapter 22

These past three nights, Eva tosses and turns before bed. We've eaten only watery soup at lunchtime. It's not easy to sleep with a grumbling belly.

"Do you know how to spell your name?" I ask softly.

"I'm too little for school." Her voice is full of regret.

I take her hand and draw a long line down her palm with three short lines running beside it. "That's an *E*. Now you draw the same on my hand."

She learns to spell her name in no time and drifts off to sleep.

I remember writing my grandparents' address on the bottom of the brown paper before I left the ghetto. Grandma's letters. Her first letter began: *We have now come to be housed in the Lodz ghetto, crowded into a basement room with three other families.* She listed everyone who was with her and Grandfather, my aunts, uncles and cousins. *There is scarcely any food to be found.* Mama read the letters aloud. She was reading to Papa, but I heard every word. My Grandfather refusing to eat, so others might survive. My Aunt Roza pregnant and losing weight. And Jakub! Each letter that followed was more terrifying than the last. Before signing her name she wrote: *Consider any letter you receive from us to be our last.*

When the morning bell rings, Eva doesn't want to wake. I'm careful not to say the word *breakfast* as I coax her out of bed.

After morning prayers, everyone's spirits lift because our

only meal of the day is next. While the others sit and wait for soup, I'm by the stove with Monika, waiting for Sister Danielle.

I listen quietly as the nuns talk. One says, "The papers were an excuse. They came here for food because they are running low. The Soviets are defeating the Germans. The occupation will be over soon."

I'm not sure about the word *occupation*. But I wonder about Germany losing. Is it possible?

An older nun responds, "The Germans know what they are doing. Poland was prepared with reinforced front lines and they plowed through. France was prepared with tunnels and barricades and they went around. They always find a way to win."

"They can't win if they can't eat," the first nun counters. I wonder if there will be a disagreement, but the conversation ends.

Monika peers into her pot as if her eyes have the strength to make her water boil. "Do you think we will have carrots or turnips?" she asks.

We only had carrots the day after the soldiers took our food. Yesterday and the day before, our meal was Sister Danielle's recipe for one-turnip soup. Turnips are more difficult to peel and not as flavorful. But they are bigger. "Maybe there will be carrots and turnips," I offer.

"Maybe Sister Danielle will find a potato."

I stare into my water and try to remember what a potato tastes like. My stomach rumbles at the thought. I can't think of the name of another vegetable so I say, "Maybe Sister Danielle will bring us winter boots."

Monika peers into her water. "Maybe Sister Danielle will bring us warm blankets and winter coats and—"

Just then Sister Danielle steps into the room and sets a wooden crate on the basin. "I'll need some help cleaning," she says. Monika and I rush to her side.

"Cabbage," says Monika. Her voice is barely above a whisper, as if she can't believe her own eyes.

"Cabbages," corrects Sister Danielle. "Two for each pot."

Sister Maria fixed the faucet the day after the soldiers destroyed it. We clean and boil the cabbage leaves. The steam from my pot of two-cabbage soup smells rich and full. It grows as it fills the room, as if the scent alone could fill one hundred bellies.

As the cabbage boils, I listen to the nuns discuss business. Three babies have found homes with local families. Much more help is needed. We are short of blankets, soap and medicine in addition to food.

When Sister Danielle excuses us to go to the dining room, Monika and I almost skip to our seats, our stomachs anxious for the taste of soup.

Klara passes by me without a word. I can't remember the last time she called me Liar. Was it when she set the bell by my bed? Has she been unkind since the soldiers were here? This constant hunger is making all of us tired and forgetful. Maybe she doesn't have the energy to start trouble.

Each day Sister Maria's prayers are stronger. She's more thankful than ever. She praises our kindness. She's certain that God is standing near us and protecting us. I pray with all my heart, with all my soul. I pray with every bit of my strength. I pray that Sister Maria is right.

Chapter 23

Something is different today. I know it before I even open my eyes. No one is talking. Most of the girls don't even sit up in bed when the sisters ring the morning bell.

"Eva, come on, up we go." She closes her eyes tightly. "Eva, please. Help me with the little ones."

Veronica says what we're all thinking, "I don't want hot water. I want food, bread."

"Girls," I say loud enough for everyone to hear, "we mustn't lose hope. We must stay strong." A few girls sit up, but none are getting out of bed.

"I don't want to," says Eva, tucking her face into the crook of my elbow.

"I guess you've never heard the story of the determined mouse who wanted a bit of cheese?" They sit up now. A few move out of their beds to sit closer.

"It goes like this:

"Once there was a little mouse who was so hungry. He was desperately hungry and weak. He searched everywhere for food, but there was none to be found.

"While searching, he smelled something—a bit of cheese, but it was way up high on a dresser and out of sight.

"So the mouse tried to climb the dresser. He made it as far as the bottom drawer and slid back to the ground. The mouse could still smell the cheese at the top so he tried again.

"This time he made it to the second drawer. And again he slid back down.

"So the determined little mouse tried again. He climbed with all of his might and he made it to the third drawer—"

"And he got the cheese," says Roza. I haven't heard her voice for days. She's chewing on the ends of her hair.

I want Roza to be right. But today is our fifth day with very little to eat. I know the mouse in my story must work even harder.

"No," I say. "He slid back down again. And this time it really hurt when he landed. Still, he didn't give up. The fourth time he climbed higher. Just past the fourth drawer. He put a little paw on the top of the dresser." The girls lean in close to me. "He hung from the very top. The cheese was so close." I pause and look around. They're wide-eyed and awake now.

"And he fell again," I say.

The girls slump back, disappointed.

"Now he knew that he could do it. He wouldn't give up. He ran up to that dresser and scrambled to that ledge. And this time, the fifth time, when he got his paws on the very top of the dresser, he pulled himself up. And there was the cheese."

"Oh, good," says Roza, swinging her legs off the edge of her bed.

"And do you know what?" I ask.

"What?"

"There was more cheese there than he expected. And a bit of cracker too."

We file down the hall and to our seats, where we find bowls of hot water waiting for us.

Chapter 24

Morning prayer service is longer than usual, longer than ever. Perhaps it's Sunday. Perhaps the nuns have nothing for us to do and see we are too weak for chores. Perhaps there are no more cabbages, turnips or carrots and they are keeping us here to distract us from the idea of lunch. Sister Maria prays loudly, but most of the girls just sit and stare. We stand to sing and no one joins in.

Many songs but few dumplings. Grandma used to say this to me and Jakub when we sang or played instead of doing our chores. He would come home from school with the best songs and after he sang them only once, I'd have the song memorized forever. *A liar must have a good memory.* I know how true Grandma's words are. Grandma would want me to be Anna Karwolska. I change the words: *A survivor must have a good memory.*

Sister Maria lifts her arms and says, "You may be seated." We plop down.

There's a tapping sound behind us, soft at first. The music stops; someone is knocking at the main door. The nun closest to the door pulls it open. It's the man with the cart, the one who brought me here months ago. Though I'm in the middle of the room, I hear the man's low, clear voice when he says, "I have brought food."

I stand with Eva and the other young children watching the older girls. They form a line to move the food from the cart to the pantry. The wind is so strong; I move Eva behind me to protect her from the gusts. We don't care about the cold or the wind. The older girls pass sacks of grain, crates of vegetables and even tins from one to the other down the long line. Monika is near the cart. Next to her, a short girl in a tattered brown dress drops a sack that's placed in her arms.

I should be helping them. Now even Anna Karwolska has been nine for many months. No one suggested moving across the hall with the older girls, so I kept quiet. I want to stay with Eva.

"I can help," I say. I rush to stand opposite the girl. We lift the small sack of grain and pass it to the girl beside us. Monika places the next sack in both our outstretched arms and we turn to pass it down the line. The girl's hair blows in front of her eyes. The wind scratches against my ears, freezes my face and pulls my braids out behind me.

When the last of the food is removed from the cart, my arms are shaking and burning. My feet are numb and pinched in my tight shoes. Sister Maria shoos us inside to warm up. There is already warm water waiting at our places. The room fills with the smell of food, real food. Lunch is porridge, so thick and delicious it fills my stomach completely. After my last spoonful, I'm sure I'll never be hungry again.

At dinner we line up for hot soup. Roza tips her bowl to her mouth and drinks it standing in line. Sister Danielle glances her way, but doesn't pause to scold her for drinking before the soup is blessed. The girl in front of me steps around her, leaving a wide space, and I do the same. I make sure to hold my soup close, in case Roza decides to make a grab for my bowl. But she's got her bowl tipped high, draining it of every last drop, and doesn't seem to notice me at all. As we're eating, Sister Danielle makes her way between the tables. She surprises each of us with a thick slice of bread.

All of the girls are quiet in the bedroom before bed. But it's a different kind of quiet than this morning. It's a full-belly quiet.

"You're missing one of your ribbons," Eva says, pulling my braids forward on my shoulders. "Your favorite special ribbons." The small pieces of Mama's shirt. I've worn them every day since we parted. There is only one now; the other must have blown away in the wind. I slide the strip of cloth off the end of my braid and rub it against my cheek.

Eva's eyebrows arch and her eyes open wide. She looks as if she might cry for my loss. "Don't worry," I say, keeping my voice strong. "Here." I hold my hand out to her. "Spell your name for me."

She writes it quickly. "Teach me yours," she says. She learns my name in a flash and snuggles close to me.

Eva breathes deeply beside me as she drifts off to sleep. I think of my cousins around the table, a holiday dinner at Grandma's house. My feet ice-cold and blurry under the water at the edge of the lake. My grandfather's hands placed ever so gently on top of my head each time he walked past me. I rub Mama's cloth against my cheek. Tomorrow I will make one large braid and tie it at the bottom. Tonight I hold the strip in my hand as I fall asleep.

Chapter 25

It's been at least a dozen days since the man brought us food. Things are nearly back to normal. There's no food to spare, but there's enough. And some things have changed. The babies have all found homes outside the orphanage, so there is more space and less noise in our room. Klara still sings the loudest during prayer service and prays while the rest of us do chores, but she calls me Anna instead of Liar and doesn't seem to notice Roza at all.

Sister Maria's prayers tell us not to fear, but we have new fears now. They are always listening for the sound of car motors and soldiers' voices. We look out the windows each time we pass, just in case they are there, ready to pounce.

The morning is silent. Sun is streaming through the windows. But the sisters haven't rung the bell. The little ones sit up and pull on their clothes. They yawn and stretch and line up by the door. Eva and I do the same.

"Do you think they are all right?" Eva asks me.

"Of course. The sisters are fine." I don't believe my own words. *Where are they? It's well past time; why haven't they rung the bell?*

One strong, high voice sings to us from down the hall. It sounds high and light like Sister Maria when the organ plays. I've never heard this song, but many of the girls know the words and start to sing along. Excitement zips through the group, flying from person to person like something real—like a butterfly.

"Do you know the song?" Eva asks.

I shake my head, disappointed for a moment. She thinks I know everything.

In a few minutes I've caught the chorus and sing along with the other girls. Sister Danielle reaches us. Her voice is beautiful.

"Little ones first," she says.

We leave the room with the youngest girls in the lead. I'm last. Across the hall, the older girls fall in line behind me. We sing as we walk. It's such a great feeling. Why don't we sing every morning?

Everyone is filing into their places instead of lining up for food. Every place has a cup, a bowl and spoon, and also a little brown ball. I stand in my place next to Eva. My hands fly to my face. It's a chestnut beside my bowl. There's one for each of us.

There's a buzz through the room. Eva smiles up at me. "Christmas," she says.

We sit down and bless the food. I reach for my chestnut. It's warm and smooth along the bottom. Rough, jagged edges curl away from the top where it was sliced.

Eva sniffs hers with a puzzled look on her face. She doesn't know how to eat it.

"I'll show you," I say. "Do what I do." I tug on an edge to unwrap my chestnut. Her eyes widen. "It's fine. Really." I pull the husk away and drop it on the table.

"You do it." She offers me her chestnut.

I shake my head. "We'll do it together." I wrap my hand over hers. "Pinch," I say, placing my fingers over her thumb and finger. "Good, now peel the hard part away." She tugs and tugs until the chestnut is unwrapped. Then she brings it to her mouth and takes a bite.

"Mmmmmmmm, it's the best food ever."

Sister Danielle is making her way around the table. She's holding a bowl in one hand and a wooden stick in the other. We all stop eating and watch her dip the stick and hold it over each girl's bowl. I watch the girls try the new addition. Their faces light up with surprise at the taste. I sit up straight and wait for Sister Danielle to make her way to me. She plops some into Eva's bowl first. "Honey," she says. And mine next. "Honey," she says again.

"Thank you, Sister Danielle," I say.

I dip my finger into the liquid. Honey. It's thick and sweet and wonderful.

Eva has her spoon in one hand and the rest of her chestnut in the other.

"Christmas," I say.

"Christmas," she agrees.

Chapter 26

"Good news," says Sister Danielle the day after the snow melts. "We will have forest days again starting today." A few girls, who have been here a long time, wiggle in their seats. "If you are new and old enough to help, go with Sister Irena. The rest, get a basket and come with me."

I don't feel new any longer. Almost a dozen girls have arrived since my first day more than seven months ago. But I've never heard of forest days, so I hurry to join the group around Sister Irena. The girls in Sister Danielle's group talk of acorns and walnuts. "Not this time of year," she says. "That was autumn. This is the start of spring."

Sister Irena leads us through the kitchen. She instructs us each to take a pail by the door. When we leave the kitchen, we don't turn to the forest with the other girls but down a path through a grassy field.

My feet feel the damp ground through the holes in my shoes. The earth squishes and my tight shoes claw into my skin with every step. In front of us is a large rectangle covered in leaves. "Line up next to me," says Sister Irena. She bends down and pushes back the leaves. Then she digs in with her hands. In a moment, she pulls out a small brown rock.

"It's a potato," she says, and drops it into her bucket.

The rest of us squat down, push back the leaves and dig in. The dirt is cool and loose. I find my first potato right away.

"Check carefully," says Sister Irena. "There could be another potato right next to the one you just found."

I reach my hand back into the cool earth and discover she's right. There's another exactly beside the one I just found. In no time our buckets are full.

We line up and wait while Sister Irena quickly checks the soil we just searched. She finds five potatoes in the dirt the smaller children harvested, but she doesn't scold them. Instead she holds each one up for all to see and says, "Look here, this one must have just sprouted."

That evening our soup is thick. Potato soup. The best I've ever tasted. When Eva and I snuggle into our bed at night, I barely have a moment to think about being Anna Bauman. *Mama. Papa.* I'm so warm. My belly is full. I fall asleep easily.

Cries. Sobs. Babies. No, not babies, children are crying. It's so loud; I think for a moment that the cribs are full again. Everyone sits up in bed.

"What is it?" Eva asks me.

"I don't know."

"Who's crying?" Eva's braver than I am, talking into the dark room.

"Outside," says someone, maybe Veronica. "It's outside."

We head out into the hall and follow our ears. The older girls are out too, barefoot, wearing only nightshirts. We walk down the long hallway full of saints, past the statue of Mother Maria and out the front door. A giant moon hangs low in the sky.

Sister Maria is arguing with a lady in a long dark coat. A line of horse-drawn carts stands in front of the door. Groups of small children stand beside the carts. They're so small. All must be younger than five. They cling to each other and sob. A few stand alone, crying.

A little girl darts into the woods.

Sister Maria interrupts her conversation to glance back at

us. "Monika," she says, "gather up the ones who ran into the woods."

Monika runs after them, the bright moon shining down to light the way.

You can't outrun the moon.

Sister Maria turns so quickly, I fear I've spoken my thoughts aloud. "Anna, please take the others back to bed." Slowly we turn around and make our way inside.

The entire day is spent tending to the new children. They need baths and their hair needs to be picked. Most of their clothing isn't fit to wear so something else must be found. They are young, three and four years old. We try to talk, to comfort them, but they only cry.

I want to ask them if they are from Warsaw, from the ghetto. Could they know my parents? Mrs. Rechtman? Halina or Marek? But I can't break my promises. I promised Mama and Papa that I would stay safe. I promised Auntie and Miss that I would remember my lessons. I promised myself that I would only be Anna Bauman alone in my thoughts at night— the only time it's safe.

That night our room holds extra cots, and mattresses are laid out on the floor. We really are stuffed ear to ear; some girls are three to a bed. The new girls are exhausted, but too tired to sleep. The moment the room becomes quiet, one child begins to cry and the others join her.

Someone begins to sing our Christmas song. Eva and I sing too. The new little girls quiet down and listen. I'm certain they'll sleep now. But each time we stop singing, the crying begins again. When the song ends again, Eva looks at me and says in a loud voice, "Anna, tell us a story."

"Yes, a story."

"A story, Anna."

"Please, a story."

I open my mouth to say I don't know a story, but I remember the mouse and the cheese. It doesn't seem like the right story for tonight. I really have no idea of a story to tell. "I'll try," I say. "But there must be no more crying so I can tell the story properly."

"*Once upon a time there was an evil king who did not like children. No one who worked at the castle or lived in the city dared have children so near the king. Those who wished to start a family moved away to the valley.*

"*But even there, the children weren't safe. Each spring, the king left his castle at the center of the kingdom to travel to his summer home. Each fall, he left his summer home to return to the castle. On these journeys, the king crossed right through the valley.*

"*As soon as they got word that the king was passing through, mothers and fathers sent every child into the forest for safety. There the children lived on berries in the springtime and roots and mushrooms in the fall. After the king's procession passed through the valley, the children returned home again.*

"*But one year, there was a war. The king was threatened by another king. As his spring procession marched toward the valley, the children ran for cover in the forest as usual. Worried about his safety, the evil king gave an order. 'This year, I will not take the valley road. Cut a passage through the forest.'*

"*The children were without the help of their parents, but they saw the king's men chopping a route through the forest. There was no time to run and no place to hide. The clever children put leaves in their hair and stuck leaves to their skin. They held their arms out straight and stood tall, pretending to be trees.*

"*The king's procession took a long time to cut through the strong forest. The children stood straight and tall. They didn't move when squirrels ran up and down their trunks, nor did they move when warblers built nests in their hair. So, by the time the king finally passed the children, he saw nothing but trees. The children were safe.*

"When the last carriage of the king left the forest, the tree children put down their weary arms. They shook the animals from their heads and began to walk home.

"But some children had become more tree than child. They could not put down their arms. They could not lift their feet. They couldn't even call for help.

"All of the other children worked to rescue the ones who had become trees. They dug the tree children from the dirt—their feet were growing roots. They knocked the tree children onto their sides and rolled them out of the forest to their homes. There they had to learn to become children again."

When I finish, the silence in the room grows. I look around. All of the children stare back at me. It is obvious they expect me to say more.

"The end," I say.

"That's not the end," says one of the new girls.

"How did they do it?" asks Veronica. "How did they learn to be children again?"

Grandma always said, *Don't ask questions about fairy tales.* I want to say this to Veronica, but the words only sound right in Yiddish. I chew my lip, considering how to say it in Polish. If I say it she may ask me to explain. I've never been able to explain Grandma's sayings.

"Tell us more," begs Veronica. Other girls too.

"It is the end," says Eva. "They got away from the king. So that's the end."

"What happened next?"

I can't believe it. The children are louder now than when they were crying.

"What happened next," says a voice, Sister Maria's voice, from the door, "is that all of the children went to sleep."

Everyone scrambles to their beds.

"Anna, see me tomorrow morning, right after prayers," says Sister Maria.

"Yes, Sister Maria," I answer.

The room is quiet at last.

Chapter 27

After morning prayer service, I walk directly to Sister Maria's office. I'm nervous but not afraid. I may be given a lecture, a verse to memorize or even extra chores.

"Anna." Sister Maria stands and walks out from behind her desk. "Last night you were talking when it was time to be quiet. I don't blame you for trying to help the new girls. Yet I think it is important for you to think about your actions."

"Yes, Sister Maria."

"Stand in front of the statue of Mother Maria. Bow your head and pray to her. Wait as long as it takes for an answer. Then come tell me what it is."

I walk down the long hall. When I reach the statue of Mother Maria, I talk to her as if she is my real mother. I whisper to her about the girls last night. "They were so tired and afraid." I make excuses. "I was only trying to help." I wish Mother Maria could answer my important questions. How long until I see Mama and Papa again? Will this war ever end?

I whisper to Mother Maria for a long time. Sometimes I bow my head and close my eyes, but sometimes I forget and stare at her face. When I have emptied out my troubles, I feel refreshed, as if a cool cloth has washed my face.

I turn to go back to Sister Maria's office but stop myself. I almost forgot to wait for an answer. Waiting is the hard part. I search Mother Maria's eyes, the face of her baby, baby Jesus.

The statue is calm and comforting, but it doesn't give me any answers.

I wait as long as I can, until looking at Mother Maria is no longer comforting. My stomach spins and I feel crowded, like I'm not standing in a large hall with a tall ceiling, but waiting under a desk in the dark.

When I knock on Sister Maria's door, she doesn't invite me in. Instead, she steps out into the hallway. "Do you have an answer?"

"I'm not sure," I admit. "Perhaps the answer came from Mother Maria. Or maybe it's something I thought up myself."

"Very well," says Sister Maria. She glances into her office. "What is your answer?"

"I think Mother Maria said that I should not spend my time making up stories. But I shouldn't spend my entire morning talking to her if I can do some useful work instead."

"Very well," says Sister Maria. "Wait here."

In the time it takes for Sister Maria to walk into her office and turn around, she's back with a dust cloth. "Clean the windowsills along the hallway and the door frames as high as you can reach."

"Yes, Sister Maria."

As I dust the first windowsill, I hear Sister Maria's conversation through her open door.

"We heard of your capture. We even received news of your death."

"In these times, one doesn't know what to believe," answers a woman. The voice is decisive, but so low. Someone used to talking in whispers. It's low and rumbly, but strong. I try to slow my breathing and quiet my heart so I can hear properly. I know that voice! *Jolanta?* My heart drums in my ears. *Could it be?*

"Perhaps the news you heard was true. Today I am Mrs. Dabrowska. Tomorrow perhaps another name. We try to be safe, though we know safety isn't always possible."

Oh, how I wish I could run into Sister Maria's office. I want to ask Jolanta a million questions. I race to the end of the hall and clean every windowsill as fast as possible. I turn and speed to each door and run the cloth over the frame, as high as I can reach. My heart pounds, my breath is short and fast, faster than my feet. Running back to Sister Maria's office, my feet almost leave the ground. I feel as if I'm running back home.

Outside the door, I hear Sister Maria say, "Fifteen will help a great deal."

"Tomorrow, then," says Mrs. Dabrowska, who sounds just like Jolanta.

I walk into the office and set my cloth on Sister Maria's desk. I study the woman. Her hair is not like Jolanta's, and something is different about the face. Could it really be her? The woman smiles at me. I've never seen Jolanta smile. "And how are you today?" She places a hand on my arm.

"Very well, thank you," I say. The hand doesn't feel familiar, but the woman's eyes do. *Does she know me?*

"Anna, please excuse us," says Sister Maria.

I leave the room and wait at the end of the hall by the statue of Mother Maria. I pray again. *Should I speak with her? Should I ask her if she's Jolanta?* I wait until the lady leaves Sister Maria's office. When I see her walking away, I decide it can't be Jolanta. The woman drags her left leg. It looks as if every step causes her pain. Not at all like Jolanta, who took short, speedy steps.

After dinner, Sister Maria stands in front of the room. "I will now call out the names of fifteen girls. When I say your name, stand beside me." Most of the names she calls are the older girls, including Klara. But near the end, Sister Maria says, "Anna Karwolska." I stand and join the others.

When we're all gathered around, Sister Maria excuses the other children. After they leave the room, she says to us, "Find Monika and ask her to give you clothes fit to travel in. Tomorrow you'll be leaving us to stay with families."

"No, no, no, no," cries Klara, covering her face with her hands. "No, not again." We all stare in shock. No one says no to Sister Maria. Klara sinks to the floor, draws up her knees and says, "Not again. Please, don't make me go. Please, don't make me go."

I take a step toward Klara and step back again. She is not the Klara I know, the girl who calls me a liar, who prays the loudest, who makes every effort to prove that she is better than the rest of us. She's trembling on the floor, nearly in tears, like the young children who arrived yesterday.

"Very well," says Sister Maria. "You'll stay here. It's for the best." She nods encouragingly to Klara. "I'll send someone in your place."

We walk slowly to our rooms. I listen to the girls whisper to each other about living with families. "There's sure to be more food," says one girl. But the rest give frightening reports about hiding in basements and inside wardrobes. One girl says she knows of a boy who was hidden under the floorboards for so long that he went blind.

I turn in a circle, staring at these girls I have known for over a year. We've eaten together, worked together, attended prayer service together. I thought they were all Catholic.

There is only one reason they would need to hide, one reason for Klara to be afraid to leave. They're Jewish, just like me.

Chapter 28

Monika declares my school uniform unfit. I know it is nicer than most anything anyone else wears. I can't speak, but my face must show that I'm upset.

"It's your outfit, Anna. You can take it with you. But you can't wear it to travel. The skirt is only to your knee." She hands me a gray dress that reaches almost to my ankles. "Here," she says, and passes me a pair of woolen tights. They are thick and soft and I want to pull them on at once. My feet have been in such pain, with my toes bent and pressing against the end of my shoes and no socks to protect my skin. But if I wear the tights, I'll never get my feet into my shoes.

"Why do you keep so much clothing here when some of the girls . . ." I stop, ready to apologize. How could I question Monika and Sister Maria? They've done nothing but help me.

"The clothes came only yesterday. Brought by someone from Warsaw." Monika bends over and searches through piles of clothes on the floor. "Take these, too," she says.

New shoes! The shoes aren't actually new, but they're big enough for my feet with room to grow. They are gray with strong straps, and worn in just enough to be comfortable but not so much as to have holes.

"Thank you."

As I turn to leave, Monika hands me a navy ribbon and adds, "Take that cloth off the end of your braid."

That night I teach Eva the whole alphabet. When she falls asleep, I hold her close. *Oh, how I will miss her.* The girls, even the newest, littlest girls, settle down quickly without crying. When all is quiet, my mind stretches out to the next day. Where will I be? Hidden in a wardrobe? Locked in a cellar? I can't imagine the future, so I close my eyes and focus on what I know is true. I let myself become Anna Bauman.

I remember playing with my cousins in Papa's shop. Hanna, Jakub and I built roads with the sawdust on the floor, an imaginary town. Jakub had a chunk of wood bigger than his hand, pretending it was a delivery truck. He smashed through the carefully constructed town. I had a small triangle, just a scrap of wood. It was easy to navigate along the curvy roads. Papa sat at his desk sketching, as a customer described a piece of furniture. Whenever customers wanted changes, Papa never became upset. He just flipped the page on his sketchbook and started again.

When I walked through town with Mama, she pointed out Papa's work everywhere. In the corner market: "Your father made those bins for Mr. Barlomie." At the bakery: "See the long display with the glass shelves? Your father made that in his shop." Even when we took Grandma to have her eyeglasses repaired. I studied the wall of small wooden drawers. Mama bent her head and whispered in my ear, "Your father made that cabinet."

The next morning at breakfast, I tell Eva. "I have to leave today. I'm going to miss you."

She climbs up on my lap and throws her arms around me. "I love you, Anna. I love you."

"I love you, too."

Just as I finish my last bite, Sister Maria finds me. "It's time to go," she says.

Sister Maria holds my hand and we walk outside. A man wearing a blue shirt stands by a horse and a small cart with two benches. There's no cover to the cart. No blanket to toss over me. I will be riding out in the open.

The man holds my elbow and helps me climb onto the front bench. I take a breath and look around. I'm closer to the trees. I can almost see over the top of the wall beside the church.

Sister Maria gives the man my papers. She reaches for my hand and squeezes it tightly. "Do well, Anna. I hope you do very well."

"Thank you."

When we reach the road, the man says, "My name is Tomasz. I'm taking you to live with my sister. So you can call me Uncle Tomasz."

"Are there a lot of children at your sister's house?"

A frown crosses Tomasz's face for a moment. "Only her son, Jerzy. He's fourteen." I turn to look back at the church. It's enormous and full of children. "My sister loves children," Tomasz continues. "She's a schoolteacher."

I close my mind and imagine myself in a classroom again. The gray dress with droopy sleeves seems out of place on me. My legs are warmed by the woolen tights and my toes have room to wiggle in my shoes. It's not only the clothes, but the odd sensation of the church growing smaller behind us. I don't feel like myself. Maybe today I'm really becoming Anna Karwolska.

I tell the man the name of Anna Karwolska's hometown. "That's where I'm from. Have you ever been there?"

"I've passed through it once or twice."

"What's it like? Is there a big river with many bridges? Is there just one church or a bunch of them? Is it near the sea?"

He looks at me a long moment and says, "Don't you know?"

I realize my mistake. I really don't know what Anna Karwolska's town is like. I wonder for a moment if Uncle Tomasz can see right through my life, past the life of an orphaned Catholic girl and into the life of a Jewish girl in hiding.

I swallow and say, "Yes, I know. It's just that I've been away so long. My old home is like something that happened a long time ago. Almost like a dream."

Uncle Tomasz nods. "I can imagine it would feel like that."

There's no lock on a mouth, Grandma would say. But I mustn't think about Grandma now. *I am Anna Karwolska. I must know the correct answers.*

Chapter 29

"Here we are," says Uncle Tomasz as we enter a small town. We turn off the main street onto a country road. Three people are standing outside the farmhouse when we pull up. Uncle Tomasz jumps down and kisses his sister on her cheeks three times. He does the same to her husband and his nephew. Excitedly, he whirls around. "And this," says Tomasz with his arms pointing up at me and a huge smile on his face, "is Anna."

I stand and say, "Hello." Tomasz helps me down and his sister holds me in a tight embrace.

"Just look at you," she says. "Just look at you. You're just as I expected." She turns to her husband. "Look at this girl, Stephan."

"I see her," Stephan answers. He doesn't smile but his blue-gray eyes are friendly. "You haven't even told her your name."

"I'm Sophia. And this is Stephan." She points first to her husband and then her son. "And this is Jerzy. You can call me Mama Sophia. Or just Sophia."

"Thank you," I say. I can't imagine calling anyone Mama besides my real mother.

Inside, Sophia serves thin slices of brown bread, carrots and flavored beans. I feel four sets of eyes on me as we eat. I try to eat slowly, but the food, and especially the milk, is so delicious. Just like at the orphanage, there's no food to spare but there's enough.

Sophia adds milk to my cup each time I set it down.

"Be careful or she'll drink so much she'll float away," Stephan teases.

I set my cup down without drinking, worried I've had more than my fair share.

Sophia smiles. "I can't help it. I want to fatten her up." She speaks with such concern, as if she were my very own Mama. I'm glad the meal is nearly over, because a lump is growing in my throat.

When the last bit of food is eaten, Tomasz thanks his sister for the meal.

"What about the family piece of bread?" asks Jerzy.

Sophia steps to the counter and returns with a small plate and a thin slice of bread. Stephan breaks the bread into five even pieces and passes one to each of us. It's only two extra bites of bread, but Jerzy smiles as he chews and I can't help thinking that these last two bites taste better than the rest.

After Uncle Tomasz leaves, Sophia says, "Come, Anna. I'll show you to your room." She leads the way up some small, dark stairs. The stairs are steep, almost like walking up a ladder. We enter the dark room and my stomach sinks. *She's taking me to a hiding place. I won't be in the open after all.*

Sophia turns on a light. There is a small bed next to the attic window, a chest of drawers with a mirror above and even a small desk. "You can place your things in here." Sophia slides open the top drawer of the dresser. She notices me looking longingly at the desk. "There's no school because of the occupation."

I just nod and place my rolled-up school uniform in the drawer. It's the only thing I have except the scrap of cloth Mama used to fasten my braid, which is tucked into one of the pockets.

Sophia sits on the small bed and I feel odd standing and staring at her, so I sit down beside her. "Were you with the nuns a long time?"

"Over a year," I tell her.

"This is all very new for you. Do you have any questions?"

I pull my hands up into the ends of my long droopy sleeves. I have a million questions. *Why am I here? How long can I stay? Does anyone in the world know my secret? And most important, when will my parents find me?* "Have you had any other orphans stay with you?"

Sophia shakes her head. "Just you, Anna, only you." And she pulls me into another hug. So many hugs in one day. So many I've lost count. When Sophia heads out the door, down the steep, dark stairs, I ask, "How long should I stay here in this room?"

Sophia turns back in surprise. "You may come and go as you please. It's your room, Anna. Come with me and I'll show you the rest of the house."

The rest of the house is small. The kitchen where we had lunch, a small living room, a bathroom with running water, and a bigger room with Stephan and Sophia's bed and a mat laid out on the floor. *Jerzy gave up his room for me.*

Best of all is the outside. Fields and trees stretch out in every direction; we're far from any other house. Stephan has three little work sheds. It's quiet. Except for the birds, everything is quiet and still. I run through the fields to the edge of the trees. How I wish there were apple trees loaded with fruit. I settle for a prickly pine and wiggle my way between the branches. They reach out from the center like a spiral staircase and I climb. Up, up, up. I climb until I see the top of Stephan's sheds. Until I see the top of the house. When I stop, I'm more than halfway up the great pine tree, standing somewhere between the earth and the clouds. When I wander back to the farmhouse, I bring some of the forest with me. Sap covers my palms, so thick it nearly glues my fingers together.

Stephan stands outside the house talking to a tall man in uniform—a German soldier's uniform! They are speaking a strange combination of German and Polish. I don't understand all of the words. There's nowhere for me to hide. *Anna*

Karwolska doesn't need to hide. As I approach, I hear the soldier thank Stephan for his help.

"You know you can count on me," says Stephan.

The soldier turns and steps directly into my path. He's so tall; I think if Stephan stretched his arms high in the air, he wouldn't be able to reach the soldier's cap. I take a step back and immediately wish I hadn't. So I step forward again.

"Who do we have here?" The giant soldier smiles down at me.

Stephan tells the soldier my name. I try to cover my fear by standing tall. I speak loudly and clearly in German. "Good evening."

The soldier's smile grows. "What a smart, polite girl you have here," he says to Stephan. He bows his head to me and says, "Good evening, miss."

Stephan holds the door and we make our way inside together. "I didn't know you could speak German," he says.

"Who was that man?"

"He's important in this town." Stephan waits, as if he knows I have more questions.

"Does he . . . do they come here often?"

"You probably didn't see many soldiers in the orphanage. But around here, they're everywhere. They like the countryside. If you can remember one thing whenever you meet a German soldier, everything will be fine."

"What?" I've remembered so much already, I can remember one more thing.

"Always be polite. The very first day they arrived, they took our livestock. I was polite and I followed directions. Since that time I've had no problems." He leans in close and sniffs. "You smell like a pine tree."

I forget about the soldier for a moment and grin. "I climbed higher than the house, almost up into the sky." I hold up my sap-covered palms.

"Climbing in trees and conversing with soldiers. Anna, is there no end to your daring?"

If he only knew. "I'm afraid of the soldiers," I admit.

"And what about trees?" he asks. "Are you afraid of them?"

I shake my head. "Only the first few times, when I was small." I remember the enormous apple tree at the park by my home.

"Still, you spoke to the soldier even though you were afraid. And that first tree, you climbed it again, enough times until you weren't afraid."

I nod.

Stephan claps his hands once, like he's just won an argument. "That, Anna, is called bravery."

Chapter 30

Sophia wakes me before the sun. "Come, Anna. Busy day ahead of us."

I dress quickly and glance at myself in the mirror. A bowl of cool water and a brush and comb are on my dresser.

Sophia and I take the last two pieces of bread with us as we walk to town.

"Where are Jerzy and Stephan?"

"Work."

"Work? But Jerzy's only fourteen."

Sophia gives me a sidelong glance as if she's surprised by my question. Then she surveys the dark road as if someone might hear her answer. "He's tall for his age. Big enough to be sent to Germany to work if he doesn't have a suitable job here." Sophia pauses and her eyes look far away. She shakes her head as if erasing a picture from her mind. "He works with a tailor, he does."

"A tailor." I like the sound of it. He takes one thing, cloth, and turns it into other things: trousers, dresses, even coats. I think of Papa's shop, the stacks of wood, machines in a large room with half a dozen men. They took ordinary-looking wood and made it into wonderful furniture.

I've never heard of people, children too, being sent to work in Germany. I should have cried like Klara to stay with the nuns. I'm not smart enough to survive out here. I don't know how to be Anna Karwolska.

"Does Stephan work with a tailor too?"

Sophia picks up her pace. "Didn't you notice his left hand?"

I shake my head.

"He hides it well. Stephan's hand was crushed when he was at the front. He has a medical excuse from working."

The sun is coming up, casting a pink light between the tree branches. Stephan was on the front lines like Papa and Uncle Aleksander and thousands of other men who tried to stop Germany from invading Poland. "But he wasn't at home when we left."

Sophia lets out a sigh and then smiles. "He . . . Stephan meets with his friends to see if anyone needs help." I think of the tall German soldier Stephan was talking to last night. *Are they friends? Is that who Stephan helps?*

When we make it to town, there's already a line in front of a building. We take our place in the back and others queue up behind us. I recognize the long, low shape of the building; it is exactly like the one I walked my cousin Jakub to for a year, where I had three days of first grade before the war. "This is a school!" I can't keep the excitement out of my voice.

"It was a school," says Sophia, shaking her head. "Now it is an administration building." I have no idea what an administration building is, but I can tell by Sophia's voice it is nothing to be happy about.

The line is made up of elderly people and young women who have small babies. Many of them glance our way. They talk to one another. I'm afraid they are talking about me. Before long, four German soldiers stroll down the block to the door of the building, unlock it and step inside. It takes over three hours to make it to the front of the line. I'm sweating as we get nearer the soldiers. There are no other children my age. I stand out too much. I shouldn't be here. What if they think I'm big for my age? What if they want to send me to Germany to work? How I wish I could work at the tailor's with Jerzy.

Fortunately, the soldier who takes my paperwork from

Sophia appears bored with his job. He asks me my name and my birthday, barely glancing my way. He hands Sophia my booklet of new ration cards, updated with Stephan and Sophia's address.

"Now let's hope that some of the shops are still open."

After four more hours of standing in line at three shops, my knees ache and my feet are sore. We make our way home with a half loaf of bread, six cabbages, three carrots and a bottle of milk.

"Don't worry, Anna," Sophia says. "Standing in line isn't the only way we can get food."

Chapter 31

Jerzy sets a big pencil and three sheets of brown paper beside me after dinner. "Go ahead, draw something." He begins sketching on his own paper. I try to see what he's drawing but he's leaning forward, blocking my view.

The house is quiet. Sophia and Stephan have gone outside. I slowly let my pencil glide on the page. A flower emerges. And a rainbow. A single star shines at the top of the paper. Soon other stars come out to fill the sky and the moon appears in the corner.

A honking sound makes me jump up from my chair. In an instant I'm under the table, shaking. Jerzy sits on the floor opposite me. He meets my eyes between the chair legs. "Anna, what's wrong?"

"That sound." I know it wasn't a car motor, but it was out of place, frightening.

"That's Old Ella, our cow. We share her between three families. She only comes out at night."

A cow? I crawl out from under the table feeling foolish.

"We keep her hidden. Or they would take her. She's still a good milker and usually she knows to be quiet." It doesn't make sense. How would a cow know to be quiet? "Do you want to go outside and meet her?"

I shake my head.

He reclaims his seat at the table and looks at my paper. I

glance at his. It's a sketch of a person, a little girl's face. She has wavy hair and her lips almost smile.

My drawing of a flower, a moon and stars is plain. The rainbow looks like the work of a first grader. I put my hand over the images, but it's too late. I trace a circle around the flower, then the rainbow and finally the stars. I know Jerzy is still watching me. My chest constricts and my throat starts to tickle. "I haven't drawn anything in a long time. My pictures remind me of a poem," I say. My throat is closing up and my voice shakes when I say, "A poem my father told me the last time I saw him."

"Tell me the poem."

"I don't remember it all. Just a few lines. I wouldn't say it right." I fold my arms and put my head on the table.

"There's no reason to be sad, Anna."

Jerzy's trying to be kind. But I want to disagree, to tell him that there are reasons to be sad, so many reasons. Instead I say, "Yes, I know."

"Do you have brothers or sisters?" Jerzy asks.

I'm surprised by the question. This is something everyone talks about, but we never practiced. Anna Karwolska is an orphan. But that only means her parents are dead. *Why does everything have to be so confusing?* I decide Anna Karwolska is an only child, like me. I look up at Jerzy and shake my head.

"You're staying with us now. So you have a brother."

I nod. I have—Anna Karwolska has—a brother.

Just then Sophia returns. Jerzy tells her that we heard Old Ella, but he doesn't mention how the cow frightened me. "And you have to help Anna find a poem," he insists.

I tell Sophia what I can remember of the poem:

"A bright flame of truth grows.
With every secret you learn.
Your soul is greater still.

"It was so long ago. There were many more words. The last line was about stars fading away." I trace my finger around the stars I drew.

"It does sound familiar," Sophia says.

"She is a teacher. She will find your poem," says Jerzy. He turns to Sophia. "It's a poem her father told her."

When Stephan joins us, Sophia makes an announcement. "Anna's been part of our family for four days now. Tomorrow we will attend church together." She looks at me and holds out her arms. "Anna, I made this for you." Sophia is holding up a beautiful dress. The white material is so new, it shines. Thin green stripes are woven into the fabric. The dress is perfect in every detail, including a tiny crisp green bow on each sleeve.

"It's beautiful," I say.

Sophia beams. "I've worked on it every night since we knew you were coming. Try it on for us."

I hold the dress carefully as I climb the stairs. It feels delicate, like something that might break. I put it on without looking at myself in the mirror. Instead, I hurry downstairs to Sophia.

"It fits perfectly." Sophia holds her hand to her heart. "Look, Stephan. Look at Anna."

"I see," he says. He's looking at Sophia, who is looking at me.

Jerzy looks up. "Nice dress."

Suddenly it feels like I've fallen and had the wind knocked out of me. I sit down on a chair. They all look at me with such attention. I open my mouth to tell them how much I like the dress, but instead I start to cry, to really cry. Their faces change from smiles to concern. I cover my face with my hands, partly to hide myself, but mostly so I won't have to look at them. I would never want to make them upset. My hands are wet. I'm actually crying for the first time in years.

"What's the matter, honey?" Sophia asks.

"It's just . . . it's just . . . ," I mumble into my hands. I'm out of words. "I can't believe I'm crying." They don't know me. Don't know that I haven't cried—not when bombs fell, not when people died, not when I left my family, not when Rachel was taken away.

"Can we help?"

I wipe my eyes, but it doesn't stop the tears. "I just . . . I feel . . . strange being part of a family again."

"I'm sure you do," says Sophia. "Come, I will help you get ready for bed. Church tomorrow."

It's dark and the house is quiet. But I don't turn back the clock and remember being Anna Bauman. Instead, I stare out the window of my new home. I think about the girls from the orphanage, the other fourteen who left the same day I did. Were they all as lucky as I? I remember Klara's scowling face, her whispers in my ear and her fear of leaving the orphanage.

I place my palm against the cool window, close my eyes and try to imagine Papa standing next to me, his finger tracing the outline of my hand. I climb back into bed. How I wish I could talk with my parents. *I'm sorry.* I take a deep breath and try to calm the feelings wiggling around in my chest. *I'm not their daughter. They are trying to make me feel like I am their daughter. How can they care about me so much after only a few days?*

They care about Anna Karwolska. But how would they feel if they knew my secret? Could they care this much about Anna Bauman? Will I ever get to be myself, my real self, again?

There are no voices inside my head. No more questions and, worse, no answers. I can't remember a time when my mind has been this quiet. Usually it is a jumble of thoughts, so many thoughts I can't keep them straight. Warm tears slip out of the corners of my eyes. After all this time without tears, I'm crying twice in one night.

Chapter 32

Before church, Sophia offers to braid my hair. As she stands behind me, crossing the strands, I close my eyes and remember Mama. I should be Anna Karwolska; it's daylight. At any moment a neighbor, even a soldier, could come through the front door and start asking questions. But Anna Bauman and especially Mama and Papa are slipping so far away from me. Sophia's careful with my hair and quiet. I try to pretend she is Mama. But Mama used to tug my hair tightly and twist it as she braided, humming to herself all the while.

Other families dot the county roads as we walk to church, strolling to the city center. We pass beside a black iron gate. Inside, tombstones stand in a line, cold and still. Something blue flashes between rows of grave markers at the other side of the cemetery. The movement is quick, like an animal. But I know I saw a blue dress. I look back at Jerzy and Stephan and up at Sophia and the lady she's chatting with, but none of them seem to have noticed.

When we turn the corner, the giant church bells start clanging and chiming.

"Right on time," says Stephan.

The church is directly in front of us. I stop when I see two soldiers standing at the front door smoking. Jerzy steps on my heels. "Sorry," he says. I walk next to him, behind his parents. *Why are the soldiers here? Do they check everyone's papers as they enter the church? Will they question me?*

We start up the walkway to the church. The soldiers are smoking and talking to each other. I hold my breath as we walk past.

After we're seated, I can't resist; I turn and look for the soldiers. They've put out their cigarettes and are walking inside, not only two but three soldiers now, all in uniform. They file in, two rows behind us. As they sit, I realize that they are here to worship, just like the rest of us. *And they will be able to watch my every move.*

Finally, Mass begins. Mass here is just like morning service at the orphanage, but they have a man nun in place of Sister Maria. The prayers are the same and the order we do things is the same. I even know the songs. I could do this in my sleep. After Mass, we make our way outside. We're instantly surrounded by more friends. After smiling for a bit, I pull on Sophia's hand. "Can I walk around the churchyard?"

She gives me a smile. "Don't go far."

I march to the far end of the cemetery where I saw the girl in the blue dress. I search all the way to the back fence, but there's nothing. I pace between the gravestones slowly, looking for clues. *Maybe I imagined it.*

As I turn to walk back to the church, something metal catches my eye. I bend down and find a small spade. Scanning the area, I notice a tiny shed tucked under a tree by the side gate. I hear shuffling inside as I approach the door. "Hello?" Only silence. "Hello?" No answer.

I push the door open. A teenage girl sits on the floor in the corner, her knees pulled to her chest. Her coat is long and gray. She's not the girl with the blue dress. She doesn't make a move or say a word, but her eyes are fixed on me.

"Hello?" I say again. I walk in hesitantly and put the spade on a table.

I hear a creak behind me and the girl's eyes flick to the door, alarmed. I turn. There's a boy of about five. His hair has grown into his eyes and he wears a long light-blue coat. The boy pulls the door shut behind him and makes his way to the girl. She stands and puts an arm on his shoulder protectively. They look alike. I decide they are brother and sister.

"Hello." I try again. "My name is Anna." I touch my chest and repeat my name. "Anna."

With each of my words they take a step back as if I'm pushing them away. So I back up until my heels hit the door, giving them space.

The girl is shaking her head, speaking softly in a language I can't understand. The boy pulls on her hand and speaks rapidly to her. I understand a few of the words he says, *food* and *luck* and *good*. But I can't manage to put it all together. She shakes her head at him and her finger at me. She's scared. The little boy's frightened too, but he has more hope, and more hunger, than he has fear.

I suddenly know why they are hiding. And what would happen to them if they were caught. And what will happen to me if I'm found with them.

I turn and put my hand on the doorknob, and a familiar memory gathers around me like a warm blanket. I know some of their words because they are speaking Yiddish.

As I pull the door open, I hear a high-pitched sneeze. I'm not sure if it was the girl or the little boy. I speak without turning around. "*Vahksin zuls du tsu gezunt.*" May you grow in health. The words my grandmother always said after a sneeze.

I rush out and pull the door closed behind me.

Chapter 33

The next day, as we walk home from the shops, I can't get my mind off the girl and boy. I wonder who is hiding them and why they picked the shed in the churchyard. It's out in the open and not even locked. It's a very poor hiding place.

Sophia tells me that many of the stores in town are closing and others will only open two days a week instead of three. "I will be spending nearly the entire day waiting in line. I'll need your help at home."

"Of course."

"We have chickens, hidden in the forest. They need to be fed and their eggs gathered."

"I can do that."

Sophia nods. "And you'll be milking Old Ella as well."

I cough. "I'm . . . I'll . . . I just . . ."

"What is it, Anna?"

"I've never milked a cow before."

Sophia chuckles. "There's nothing to it."

"I've never even seen a cow before."

This stops her in her tracks. "What's this nonsense? Of course you've seen a cow. Everyone has seen a cow." I shake my head. She sighs. "There used to be cows everywhere." Sophia looks out into the distance. "And pigs and chickens too. Not to mention at least five times as many horses pulling carts. Had to really watch our step if we were on foot." She's talking about before the war. Like Papa. "We didn't stand around trading three eggs for ounces of butter, either. Or pull apart a sweater in order to have yarn to knit new socks."

At home we find Old Ella in the small shed, and Sophia instructs me in milking. There isn't much milk at first and Sophia closes her fingers around my hand to help. Old Ella helps by staying quiet and standing still. Each little squirt of milk adds to the pail. When we're finished, my fingers are tight from the effort and Old Ella has provided half a pail of rich white milk.

Stephan and Jerzy come home soaking wet and there hasn't been a drop of rain all day. Sophia doesn't even ask about it, but I do. Stephan just slides into his room and closes the door. Jerzy gives me a quick glance and says, "Work."

"At the tailor's? You got wet making clothes?"

Jerzy looks to his mother for help.

"Anna, listen. Jerzy and Stephan, their work is . . . complicated. They help a lot of people. It is best if we don't ask any questions, do you understand?"

I don't understand, but I say, "Yes."

"Come, Anna," says Sophia. "There's something I must show you."

I follow her up the stairs to my room. Sophia pulls my dresser away from the wall. There's a small door behind it. Sophia crawls in on her hands and knees and pulls out a few books. They are all the same, thin schoolbooks with a light brown cover. Sophia stands and dusts off the top book. I kneel down and look in the little room. It is packed full of books. There must be over a hundred, maybe over two hundred.

"I saved them from the fire." Sophia says. "The night before they closed the school, we snuck the books out, every single one. I can't tell you how many houses in town have hiding places like this stuffed with books."

"Fire?"

"The Germans made a law that schoolbooks could not be written in Polish. They burned every schoolbook they could find." Sophia shakes her head. "As soon as this war is over, we'll be ready to open the school doors again." Sophia hands me a thick book with a light green cover. "I'm not sure, but this one might have the poem you are looking for."

Papa's poem. It has been so long since I've held a book in my hands; I hug it to my chest. There were so many books at my old house. Jakub would stack them high enough to make a fort. Hannah and I played school every day. Before I could read, I used to open books and tell stories aloud. Once Mama caught me turning the pages of her expensive music scores. I had insisted I was reading a fairy tale to the cat.

Before bed, I pull open my top drawer, reach down into the pocket of my skirt and find the strip of cloth Mama used to tie my braid so long ago. I run it though my fingers and rub the silky cloth against my check. I close my eyes and imagine my parents standing beside me. After a moment, I tuck the cloth away and close the drawer.

I bring the book to bed. It is a type of schoolbook for older students, with pages of explanation and poems scattered through every chapter. I turn to the list of poems in the back and try to read the titles. But I don't know the title of the poem Papa recited. Just that it had stars and flowers and a rainbow and it was about—what was it about? Hope? Time?

It is impossible for me to read the titles. I can't keep the words in my mind. I keep thinking of two frightened faces hiding in a tool shed. I can still feel the girl's large, worried eyes on me and hear her little brother's hopeful words. I shouldn't have spoken to them, not in Polish and certainly not in Yiddish.

Chapter 34

I've turned every page in the book Sophia gave me, but it's no use. I need help with some of the words. Sophia and Stephan are outside. I find Jerzy sketching and ask him to help me. We climb the stairs and I show him the book Sophia gave me yesterday.

"I learned to read early," I tell him. "My cousin was a year older. Each day when he came home from school, I wanted to do homework too." I worry that it sounds like I'm bragging. "But I really only went to school a few days. Then the war started."

"And everything else was more important," Jerzy says.

"Yes." Everything else for me, for my family, was bombs and moving to the ghetto. I wonder if things were ever that bad here. Did this small town get bombed? But I can tell by the way Jerzy said *everything else* that he doesn't want to talk about the war. "This book of poems is for older students and some of the poetry words are old-fashioned. My first readers had lists of words in the back with definitions, but this book doesn't."

Jerzy nods. He pushes aside the dresser and crawls into the small storage room. He backs out with three books and hands them to me. Before he closes the door, I see a familiar book and reach out to grab it. "*Elementarz!*"

"That one is too easy."

"It was . . . my cousin had one and I did too. This book taught me to read." I hug it to my chest as Jerzy covers up the storage room.

Stephan calls from the bottom of the stairs. "Jerzy, you're needed down here."

He turns to me before he leaves. "Good luck finding the poem."

I smile. I want to hug him. Sophia's hugged me hundreds of times, and Stephan a few times too. But not Jerzy. Not yet. I smile instead. "Thank you."

Stephan calls for Jerzy again. "You're welcome," he says, and hurries down the stairs.

Though it's early, I take the *Elementarz* to bed with me. I can't take my eyes off the paper cover, the bold black letters. I feel as if I'm holding a part of my home, my real home, in my hands. When I open the book, a small photograph slides out. A girl about six sitting next to an older boy. Their faces are nearly identical. The girl has round eyes, a full smile and dimples. The boy is Jerzy. I tuck the little photo up my sleeve and head downstairs. He's not in the kitchen or the living room. "Jerzy?"

Sophia comes up behind me and startles me. "They're . . . out. Off to work."

"At night?"

Sophia shrugs. "Can I help?"

I shake my head and uncross my arms. The photo falls to the floor. She bends down and studies it. Sophia sinks into her chair. Her face has turned white. It makes her lips stand out on her face, they're blood red and her eyes are dark and far away. "Lidia, my sweet Lidia."

"I'm sorry," I say quickly. "I found it in a book. I was going to ask Jerzy . . ." I step closer.

Sophia points to the photo. "That's Jerzy, see? He was about eight—no, nine. This was the first week Lidia started school. She was so proud to finally be going to school, like her brother."

I lean in and study the photo. Wispy hair surrounds Lidia's face and reaches down past her shoulders. "She was light," says Sophia. "Hair, skin, everything. Eyes gray and round like

111

Stephan's." She runs her finger along the edge of the photo. "If I had known"—Sophia is close to tears—"I would have dyed her hair black. Or kept her home from school. I would have done anything to save her."

"Save her from the bombs?"

Sophia stands up and glares down at me. "Lidia's not dead. She's *not* dead!"

I look away, shaking. Every bone in my body is rattling against the next.

"I'm sorry, Anna. Folks around here say we have to forget about the little ones. After so much time. But I won't forget about Lidia. And I know she's alive. I know she is."

Sophia sinks down into her chair again.

I nod, afraid to ask any more questions. Terrified of making Sophia even more upset.

"They took Lidia, took our children," Sophia continues. She swears about the Germans again and again. I count five swear words. "All the children who looked like their master race, they put them on a bus to Germany." Sophia sets the photo down on the arm of the chair and covers her eyes. "They won't get away with this. They won't get away with anything."

I throw my arms around Sophia's neck and press my face into her shoulder. My chest feels like it is full of river water, cold and swirling. Sophia's arms are around me, but she must be wishing it were Lidia in her lap. The same way I long for Mama and Papa to hold me.

The storm swirling in my head stills for a moment and I have a clear, bright thought. Stephan and Sophia aren't working with the Germans. If they learn I'm Anna Bauman, they may not like me as much as they like Anna Karwolska, but they'd never turn me in to the Germans, not in a hundred million years.

Chapter 35

I thought I was the first one awake, but as I climb high in the pine tree, I notice Stephan walking between the sheds with a tall girl. She hands him an envelope and walks down the road alone. I reach Stephan before he goes back inside. He jumps when he sees me. "Anna, I thought you were asleep. I wish I had known. There was someone here, a friend. I know she would have liked to meet you."

"A friend?"

"She visits about once a month, if possible. I will introduce you next time." I wait for him to tell me more, but instead he tucks the envelope into his pocket and walks inside.

Old Ella doesn't move when I step into the shed. I talk softly to her as I start to milk. I try to push and squeeze and pull just like Sophia showed me, but without her hands over mine, I'm out of sync. It's not working. I try for several minutes before I give up. I sit back and brush my hair away from my face. A few drops of milk spill into the bucket. I milk again, pulling harder now, but after twice as much time, Old Ella doesn't even give half the milk she did yesterday.

The chickens are excited to see me. I unfold the heavy cloth, dump the bucket Sophia keeps by the door, pouring out crumbs and food scraps. They peck around my feet happily. I bend to stroke the silky feathers of a golden-orange hen.

We have six eggs today, which is good fortune. Sophia has instructed me to try to trade if we have more than four eggs. I thank the chickens and secure their coop. At home, I put the basket of eggs on the table. I remove two eggs, tucking them into my pockets.

In town, as I approach the soldiers sitting at the café, I let my arms swing loose, fingers open, so they can see I have nothing to hide, nothing worth taking.

Sophia said I should try to trade eggs for vinegar or beets—beets! And to do my best to hear if anyone has meat. She gave directions to today's trading place, the third house past the administration building. Instead, I walk through the cemetery, straight to the shed, and open the door. The girl is sitting in the corner with her knees pulled to her chest. Her gray coat is over her shoulders like a cape. She lifts her head to look at me, but doesn't make a sound.

Like before, the little boy enters behind me and closes the door. He crosses the room and sits in front of the girl, setting the dirty spade beside him.

I take an egg out of my pocket and put it on the floor close to them. "*Ay*," I say. "Egg."

The boy pounces on it and closes both of his hands around it. The girl sits up straighter.

I hold up the other egg. "Egg," I say.

The little boy stands and reaches for it. "Egg," I repeat, pulling it back.

"*Ay*," he says.

"Yes, that's right. Egg."

He looks at the girl. She nods. "Egg," he says.

I place the second egg in his hands and he gives it to the girl. I watch them crack and drink the raw eggs, spilling not a drop. When they finish, they look up at me. I point to myself and say, "Anna."

The boy points to his sister and says, "Zina," then to himself and says, "Jozef." They both start speaking rapid fire. I can't understand and I don't know how to say that in Yiddish.

So I say what I know. I repeat Grandma's sayings. "Better

an egg today than an ox tomorrow." They nod. Still waiting. "Don't rub your belly when the fish is still in the lake." They look at each other. I offer another saying. "If you lie on the ground you cannot fall."

Then I remember one about a grandmother. "If my grandmother had a beard, she'd be my grandfather." I shrug my shoulders and say *grandmother* a few times.

The girl brings her fingers to her mouth. She looks at me with questioning eyes.

I shake my head. "No, I have no more food." I say it in Polish, but her eyes tell me that she understands.

Jozef reaches into his coat pocket and pulls out some dirt and hands it to his sister. Zina looks closely at it and passes something—a long string—back to him.

I scoot closer and see plump worms, one in each of their hands. They pop them into their mouths. I should look away, but I stare fascinated as they chew. For the first time I wonder if they are alone here, eating only insects and worms.

At home I tell Sophia that I arrived at the trading house too late. "No one was there," I say.

She puts a hand on my shoulder. "Well, that's two more eggs for us."

I lift my head to meet Sophia's eyes and then look down. "I—I—I . . . I dropped the eggs," I say quickly. "I dropped the eggs and . . ." I'm out of words. My heart is punching me in the chest. I'm crying. My hands feel heavy as I lift them to my face. I can't catch my breath.

"Anna, Anna," Sophia murmurs. "Anna, calm down. It's a challenge but we always find enough food to eat and the energy to fight on another day."

Why did I tell her there were two extra eggs? I should have said we had only four eggs today. Still crying, I rush out of the room.

Run from tall tales and secrets as you would run from ghosts.

I run outside and see Stephan and Jerzy making their way home, so I stop sniffling and circle back to help Sophia with the soup. They enter as we are setting the table. We each have a bowl of soup and a slice of bread. The family slice sits on a small plate in the middle of the table, waiting for Stephan to divide it after the meal.

"We have trouble," Stephan says.

I place four spoons on the table. "Better trouble with soup than trouble without soup," I say without thinking. I freeze a moment, wondering if I've spoken in Polish or Yiddish. Grandma's sayings are pouring out of me faster than the wind.

Stephan continues as if I haven't spoken and Jerzy sits down beside him.

"Paper," Stephan says. "They got our paper man. Today we had to move the whole operation."

Chapter 36

I listen quietly as Stephan and Sophia talk about the person captured, moving equipment and a desperate need for paper. Jerzy's hand is wrapped in blue cloth. When he sets his spoon down, I notice blood seeping through the bandage.

Sophia stands and begins pacing. "We don't have anything left to trade." She looks around the room. "We have nothing."

Stephan shakes his head. "I wouldn't risk it now, even if we had cash. It's not safe to be bartering for paper when they've caught our supplier."

Just then there's a knock on the door. Before anyone can answer, the door opens and the tall German soldier lets himself in. He smiles at us all and takes Sophia's vacant seat at the table.

Jerzy quickly hides his injured hand under the table and sits still as stone.

Stephan stands and pours a drink. The soldier stares at our empty bowls. He helps himself to our last piece of bread, the family slice, and starts a conversation with Stephan about Resistance fighters. "They're hanging like flags in Warsaw. Twelve of them just this morning. It's a public display, a warning. It seems these people in the Resistance don't value their lives."

I keep my eye on the piece of bread in his hand. It's gray and hard, bread earned by Sophia standing in line and trading ration tickets. The slice of bread we always share. The man turns the bread in his hand, crumbling it slowly.

"Well, good thing you're out in the country," says Stephan. "Never any excitement here."

The soldier pours his drink down his throat. "Still, they're sending me thirty more men. Must find billeting." He stands and Stephan does too.

They walk through every room of the house. "I'm sorry my home is so small," Stephan says, his voice regretful.

"No matter," says the German soldier. "You help in other ways."

Stephan stands tall. He takes in a small breath and holds it, waiting. I can imagine him in uniform, like Papa. He looks like a soldier waiting for battle.

"Do you know anyone capable of printing?" The soldier bends forward to Stephan.

"No." Stephan shakes his head. "Do you need help printing?"

The man taps his glass and Stephan rushes to fill it.

"Just the opposite." The soldier puts his hat on his head. "Trying to catch another traitor."

When the door closes behind him, we are silent for several long minutes. Then Sophia scoops up the bread crumbs the soldier crushed and drops them into the pail by the door.

Stephan begins pacing.

"How much paper do you need?" I ask.

Stephan holds up his finger and thumb to indicate the size of the stack. I rush upstairs. In a few moments, I come down with a piece of blank white paper in my hand. I hold it up for Stephan. Sophia and Jerzy look our way. "I could get you 220 of this size and about 80 more a little smaller."

Stephan's silent a moment, turning the paper over, sniffing it. "Where did you get this? And how do you have so many?"

"From the books." I turn to Sophia. "The schoolbooks. There is a blank page at each end of every book."

Sophia gathers sharp knives for each of us and we climb the stairs to my bedroom. Sophia slides the stacks of books out from behind my dresser and the four of us open the books and remove the blank pages. After a few minutes I ask, "What's the paper for?" Sophia and Stephan exchange a long glance. I'm afraid they won't answer and a bit afraid to find out, but I ask again. "What are you printing?"

Jerzy simply says, "The truth." He shrugs. "The Germans have their newspapers, full of lies. The Polish people need newspapers too. Ones that tell the truth."

"A Polish newspaper?" I remember before the war my father bought a paper every morning. Mama would complain that he left the pages everywhere, on the dining table, on the sofa, even in the bathroom.

"An underground newspaper," Stephan confirms. He cuts a back paper out of a textbook. "Not a word about this to anyone," he says.

I nod. I wish I could tell Stephan he need not worry. I'm an expert at keeping secrets. It's difficult to swallow around the lump in my throat. I blink to focus on the page in front of me. My biggest secret, I'm keeping even from them.

"I almost forgot, this came for you today," says Sophia, handing Stephan an envelope. It's a letter from his sister, who lives in another small town sixty kilometers away. He reads it aloud. It begins like any normal letter. She complains that it has been too long since she's received a letter or a visit. "*If my own nephew, Jerzy, were to walk through my door I might not recognize him after all this time.*" She reports that everyone is healthy. What comes next isn't ordinary. She tells about a family on the other side of town. Stephan's voice slows.

"*The Vila family was shot last night. All five of them, taken out and shot in front of their home. Their bodies were left in front of the house for all to see. They hid a Jewish man and his daughter. No one in town imagined they had the two hiding there, and for years at that. Somehow, they were discovered. Seven lives, taken all in a matter of minutes.*"

She ends her letter by begging Stephan to write back. Immediately, he heads out to the work shed to compose a letter. Jerzy follows him. I help Sophia stack the papers and hide the books in the storage space. I watch Sophia walk down the stairs and I feel a panic in my chest when she steps out of sight.

The air in the room is thick; it takes extra effort for me to breathe. If anyone discovers the truth about me, Sophia, Stephan and Jerzy could all be shot. I should run away, far away.

I wish I could write a letter to my parents and ask for help.

I should tell Sophia and Stephan the truth. Then they could decide if they want me to stay here or go back to the orphanage.

"Jerzy," I call down the stairs. I try to make my voice calm.

"Yes?" He hurries into my room.

I look into his face. I remember the night he told me he was my brother. Without looking away, I say, "I have to tell you something. A secret."

Chapter 37

Jerzy and I decide to leave early in the morning, before his parents wake up. "If they wake and we're gone, they'll just think we're milking Old Ella or down at the chicken coop."

I nod. It's a good plan.

"Be ready," he says as he closes my door.

I stay up late looking out my window. I think of all the time Mama spent teaching me to be Anna Karwolska. The days Auntie and Miss spent helping me learn about being Catholic. The papers, real true papers, provided by Jolanta. And how the time in the orphanage helped me learn how to behave in a Catholic church.

The moon is bright. A full round moon, like the moon on the night the small children were brought to the orphanage. It is the same moon. It only looks different. The moon keeps changing, day by day, shrinking and growing large. It pays no attention to the Earth being torn apart by war.

Grandma used to say, *If everyone pulled in the same direction the world would topple over.* But people are pulling against each other. And the world has toppled over. The world is upside down. *Oh, Grandma!*

I stare at the moon until my eyes blur. I want to go back to the time before the world toppled over, back to Warsaw before the bombs. Back to living with Mama and Papa. I climb into my bed and close my eyes, but I can still feel the moon, large and full, outside my window.

In the morning, Jerzy and I slip out without a sound. As we walk through the fields, I'm sure he can hear my heart pounding. It rings in my ears louder than the church bell. I walk straight and tall with purposeful steps, but there is a scream building in my chest.

Don't be scared if you have no other choice, Grandma used to say. I've thought of everything and I have no other choice.

Jerzy pushes the small gate and it screeches as it scrapes across the concrete. There is no other sound, not even a rooster. I lead the way down the path, wondering if there is a better option. I shouldn't put Jerzy in danger. Should I talk to the priest? Is there any way to contact Sister Maria?

Mama's pleas buzz in my ears. *Anna Karwolska would never play with a Jewish child. She'd never help a Jewish person. She hates all Jews.* I'm not Anna Karwolska. I never have been. I stand at the door of the shed. The church is hidden behind the trees. No one can see us here.

"Are you sure this is the place?" Jerzy asks.

"I've seen them here twice," I say.

I push the door open. Zina is sitting in her corner. Jozef is huddled next to her. He puts an arm up over his eyes, though it is still dark outside. Zina pulls Jozef into a tight hug. She looks at Jerzy and starts whispering softly.

"It's fine," I say. "He's my brother. We're going to take you someplace safe. Safer."

Zina's eyes dart between me and Jerzy, afraid.

I point to the door and to Jerzy. Zina shakes her head. She whispers again, rapid fire.

"What language are they speaking?" Jerzy asks

"How would I know?" I raise my voice. "There are a thousand languages in the world. And I don't know this one." Even though I told Jerzy about Zina and Jozef, I didn't tell him all my secrets. I didn't tell him about Anna Bauman.

Zina's still whispering. Now she's pointing to the door. She wants us out.

"Try French, Anna," Jerzy says.

I try to remember French. I know children's songs. I know Anna Karwolska's address. I could ask Zina her name or the time of day. I have no use for this information, but I try anyway. "What is your name?" I ask Zina in French.

She's silent a moment. I ask again. She shakes her head, doesn't understand.

I have no choice. "*A shitkel mazel iz vert merer vi a ton gold,*" I say. *A little bit of luck is better than a ton of gold.* Zina nods her head; she understands.

"What language was that?" Jerzy asks.

"Something I know in French," I say. I repeat the sentence several times, pointing to Jerzy each time I say the word *luck.*

"It sounds more like German," he says.

I point Jerzy to the door and motion for Zina and Jozef to follow. We leave the cemetery by the side gate, far from the church, and make our way toward the forest. Jerzy told me last night that there is a group of fighters in the forest, fighting for Poland. They have food and shelter. Zina and Jozef will be safer there. Stephan and Jerzy go into the forest almost every day. Jerzy has promised to check on them.

When we're hidden in the trees, Jerzy turns to me. "Go home, Anna."

"No, I'm coming with you."

Jerzy shakes his head. "You can't. It's not safe. My parents would never forgive me."

I can hear in his voice that he won't change his mind. He would leave Zina and Jozef here before he would let me come into the forest with them. If I argue it will only slow us down. "It's not safe for me to walk through town. What if I'm stopped?"

"If you're stopped, say that your mother wanted you to be

first in line for food, but you forgot the ration cards at home."
My stomach turns to ice at the thought of being stopped by the
Germans. "You can do it, Anna. Tell about the ration cards
and walk straight home."

I hug Jerzy and turn to Zina and Jozef. "*Vahksin zuls du
tsu gezunt*," I say, although no one has sneezed.

Chapter 38

A few days later, Stephan asks me to join him and Jerzy after breakfast. "Be sure to wear your coat," he says. The thin coat I brought with me from the orphanage barely fits; the sleeves don't reach my wrists.

"It's not safe for Anna," says Sophia. "Let her stay here."

"Jerzy and I will keep her safe. We need her help."

Listening to Sophia and Stephan arguing about me makes my stomach bend and twist. Their words push up against each other and remind me of my parents' voices in the ghetto, the days before I left. Sophia bundles me up as if I were small. She winds a scarf around my neck, tucking it inside my coat. She kisses me three times on my cheeks.

We walk away from town. I wonder why Stephan asked me to come along. I know now that Jerzy doesn't work at the tailor's. He tells everyone that, and has the necessary papers to avoid trouble. Like me with Anna Karwolska's papers. We take the country roads, even cut across some fields. Stephan and Jerzy turn their heads, scanning the area. It reminds me of Miss, when we left the courthouse. I asked Sophia what Stephan does when he goes on his long walks. "He's making the rounds," she told me. "Talking to people. Finding out what's going on."

We come to a small farmhouse. Stephan calls out a greeting, "It's us!" and walks through the front door. Inside the kitchen, a lady is feeding three small children.

She brings her hand to her chest when she sees me. "I was only expecting the two of you," she says. Then she shakes her head as if the sight of me disturbs her still. "He's out back."

Outside, Stephan and Jerzy hurry to a small shed. As we get near, the building sounds as if it is spinning. Stephan opens the door and Jerzy and I follow him inside. The noise is so loud I clench my teeth. The room smells of oil. A man is bent over a large machine, turning a handle. Small papers, barely bigger than my hand, tumble out the end of the machine into a box.

The man notices us and stands. The machine quiets. "You're here," he says. He wipes his hands with a cloth. Jerzy carries three boxes to a table beside the machine. "Here's how we do it," he says. Jerzy shows me how to fold the papers in half and set them inside each other to make a small booklet. I catch on just in time because the machine starts up again. The noise bounces off the walls and pounds right into my ears.

Stephan stands near the window, reading the paper while the man feeds more sheets into the machine.

The paper I hold in my hand is one we removed from the books in my room. I can read a lot better than only a few weeks ago since I have been learning new words every night searching for Papa's poem. I read the headlines printed on the first page.

POLISH GOVERNMENT IN EXILE FUNDS PATRIOTS

GERMANY SUFFERS DEFEAT AFTER DEFEAT IN THE UKRAINE

I almost drop the paper when I read the next headline: POLISH HOME ARMY FIGHTS GERMANS IN WARSAW

Warsaw. Home. Could the Polish army really push the Germans out of the city? I work as fast as I can, anxious to ask Stephan about this news. The machine stops and Stephan lays his coat next to the newspapers on the table. He unzips the lining and begins stacking the papers inside his coat.

"How do I look?" he asks when he puts his coat on. "Can you see anything?" Jerzy walks around his father, inspecting the coat, so I do the same.

"I can't see anything," I say.

"Looks good," says Jerzy.

There are six stacks of papers on the table with long strings next to them. Stephan nods to us. "Tie those in bundles. I'll be back."

We quickly tie the papers. Stephan returns with a basket of old rags. "Put the papers under here. Don't take them out until I tell you, understand?" We both nod. We take a long route home, circling the town on country roads. Stephan stops every so often and unzips the lining of his coat. He leaves newspapers in the strangest places: between logs in a woodpile, tucked beneath leaves in a wheelbarrow, under a rock.

"How will anyone find them?" I ask.

"They'll find them," says Stephan.

"The newspapers. Are the headlines true?"

"Every word," says Stephan. "Straight from the Polish government in London."

I walk between Stephan and Jerzy and gather my courage. "So there really is fighting in Warsaw, against the Germans?"

"Yes. The Polish Home Army is fighting for the city. They instructed the Germans to surrender. This is the turning point. The Germans are losing the war."

The Germans are losing the war. I repeat that sentence in my mind a few times. It doesn't seem possible. Germany has been in control of Poland for so long. They've always been bigger, stronger. "And the ghetto? The Warsaw ghetto?" I ask.

Stephan stops walking and looks down at me. "How do you know about the ghetto?"

"I . . ." Warning bells go off inside my head. I could never be afraid of Stephan. It would be such a relief to finally tell. The words sit on my tongue: *I used to live there.* The words grow heavy, but I can't push them out of my mouth. I have to say something. "A girl in the orphanage told me about it," I lie.

"Ah," says Stephan. "Everyone in Warsaw knows about the

ghetto. They were the first to fight the Germans. The Germans burned it to the ground, flat. That's when the rest of Warsaw stood up to fight."

Burned it to the ground. Flat.

"Your face," says Jerzy. "Anna, what's wrong?"

Stephan starts walking again. "I'm worrying you. Please don't think about it, Anna. Warsaw is far from here. The Polish Home Army is sure to win."

I walk along, scanning the fields like Jerzy and Stephan. "But the other papers down by the shops. They say that the Germans are winning the war. That they are in Finland. Moving into India."

Stephan waves his hand in the air as if he's swatting at a fly. "Lies. It's what they want us to believe."

We continue into town. After a few minutes, Stephan looks down at me. "Is that basket getting heavy?" It is, but I shake my head.

He leans against a fence and pulls a large ball of string out of his pocket. "I say it's time we lighten the load." He points to black birch tree next to the fence. "Do you feel like climbing?"

I nod my head. The closest branch is far out of reach. He passes the string to Jerzy. "Tie that to a bundle of papers." He looks at me. "Up you go," he says. "On my shoulders." He hoists me up high and Jerzy passes the bundle of papers to me. I wind the string around my wrist and stretch for the first branch. Once I'm up, the climbing is easy. I glance down and see Stephan and Jerzy standing back to back: lookouts.

"Not too high, Anna," Stephan calls up. "Right there is good."

I loop the string over a branch and drop the ball of string down to Stephan. I wait for Jerzy to tie the other end to the fence, then I release my hold on the papers. It works; the newspapers are hidden but easy to find.

We repeat the process five more times. The other trees are pines and easy to climb. As I step up the ladder-like branches

I'm hidden by the needles. I know the string will lead me back. Stephan and Jerzy are below, waiting. Each step I take I'm taller, stronger and somehow older than just a moment before.

At home, Sophia has warm soup waiting for us. I drink mine and go to bed early. I need time alone in my room to think. Two papers. One says Germany is conquering the world. The other says Germany is losing. The Warsaw ghetto, burned flat to the ground. So many buildings. Such a crowded place. Mama. Papa. Oh, how I want to tell them about the newspapers and me climbing high in the trees to hide them. They must be out of the ghetto, like me. They couldn't have been there.

Before I fall asleep, Sophia comes in to check on me. She fusses over me and feels my forehead again. "Are you feeling well?"

"I'm fine," I tell her. "Why do you keep asking?"

"Last night you were calling out. I came to your room. You must have been having nightmares. I held your hand. You were talking in your sleep."

This can't be. I'm Anna Bauman every night before I fall asleep.

"Do you want me to sit beside your bed tonight?"

"No, I feel fine. Really." Her footsteps are soft as she heads down the stairs. I stare at my ceiling. Now I can't even trust myself to sleep.

Chapter 39

I rub Old Ella's nose and talk to her as Sophia milks. The cow's warm breath tickles my neck and makes a cloud in the cool morning air. She'd been staying with the two other families for weeks. "I've missed you," I tell her. "I've missed your good milk."

Next we check on the chickens but there isn't a single egg to be found. Sophia sighs as we walk home. "They need more food, better food. Like the rest of us."

As we leave the shed, we see Stephan walking to the house with a woman. She's older than Sophia and has a lot of dark black hair. "Anna," he calls out. "This is the friend I wanted you to meet from Warsaw. Her name is—" Stephan looks to the lady as if he's just forgot her name.

The lady smells like bath perfume and flower petals. She reaches out to hug me and kisses my cheeks three times. "Anna, how are you?"

"Fine." I smile to hide my confusion. This is not the same lady that I saw from the tree, the one Stephan said he wanted me to meet.

Sophia tries to invite the woman in for a meal, but it is an odd time, so soon after breakfast and so long before lunch. The lady shakes her head at Sophia's suggestion, saying that she has another appointment in town. I wonder if she leaves because she knows we don't have food to spare.

Inside, Sophia presents me with a brown canvas bag;

embroidered flowers cover the outside. "You'll need this today," she says. "We're going to town to visit some of the other teachers." She rummages through the drawers in the kitchen. "And this, too." Sophia hands me a small, sharp knife. I slip it carefully into the bag.

As we walk to town, she tells me her plan. "I'll mention the poem you are looking for and ask permission for you to search through the books. They have stashes of books, like we do. When we leave the room, you cut out the blank pages in the books, like we did at home."

I walk a few paces in silence. "Shouldn't we just ask them for the paper? Maybe they will help—"

"Remember what Stephan said? Not a word of this to anyone."

I reach out to hold her hand. "Yes, I remember."

"Anna, how can I say this? They are my friends but it is difficult these days to know who to trust. Difficult to know who would help us and who would turn us in. We must have paper. And we must try to stay safe. Understand?"

I squeeze her hand tightly. I know exactly what she means.

The first home we arrive at has a sign on the door. It's a notice stating that someone in the house is quarantined for lung disease. Sophia lifts her hand to knock, but changes her mind. As we walk away from the house, Sophia shakes her head. "Clever. They're probably not sick at all."

"But the sign."

Sophia nearly smiles. "It's a sign I wouldn't mind posting on my front door, with so many German soldiers determined to live wherever they please."

At the next home, Sophia's friend greets us with a smile that grows when she learns we are in search of a poem. "Finally, someone seeks me out to discuss literature. It seems the only books anyone reads these days are ration booklets." She's determined to help me find the poem. "Say it again, girl."

I recite the words:

"A bright flame of truth grows strong
As secrets are uncovered.
Your soul is brave and expanding."

I look away from her happy face because it feels like I'm showing off. My voice doesn't shape the poem the way Papa's voice did that night by the window. "I'm not sure those are the correct words."

"Maybe Norwid," the teacher says. "Or Asnyk. They're from the same time period."

Sophia complains of her aching back and the two ladies finally leave the room. I flip each book cover and run the knife along the blank pages, slipping them quickly into my bag. I know the pages are blank. And I'm not harming the book. Still, it feels like I am stealing.

I stack the books to the side after I cut the pages out. When I have only three books left, I sense someone watching me. I lift my head and stare into the face of a small boy.

"Henry," he says.

"Anna," I answer.

His eyes are on my knife. He's about four or five years old. I offer him a blank page. "This fell out of my book, would you like it?"

He shakes his head, his eyes still on the knife. I consider crunching the paper into a ball and tossing it out of the room, but chances are he'd stay here or run right back. Finally I say, "My mother is here. I'm sure she has a surprise for you."

Without giving me another glance he hurries out of the room. I remove the second page and set the book aside. Before leaving the room, I make sure all the blank pages are tucked down deep into my bag, and reach for the two books I haven't cut.

I find Sophia searching her pockets for a surprise. "I must have left it at home and will certainly bring it next time."

"May I please borrow these two books?" I ask. "I think I would enjoy reading them, even if I can't find the poem."

"You'll find it, Anna." Sophia's friend smiles. "You have determination, I can tell."

When we turn the corner, Sophia takes a deep breath.

"He saw the knife," I say. "He saw the knife and he wouldn't leave the room."

Sophia chews her lip. "Don't worry, Anna. We have the paper. No more about this until we are home."

At home she boils water. I wonder if there are any vegetables for soup.

Sophia surprises me by bringing a steaming cup to the table. "Only one to share between us, but I found some tea I'd been saving." She pushes it in my direction and I take a tiny sip.

"There are two reasons the newspaper is so important. First of all, it brings hope. Everyone needs hope, especially now." She takes a sip of the tea and then another. "But more importantly, it saves lives." She pushes the teacup toward me and I drink. I watch her face change as she speaks, from concern to determination to excitement. "There are so many people, good Polish people who are desperate. They see a future with Germans in charge, so they switch sides. They want to join the winning team." Sophia's eyes meet mine and I believe every word she says. "They need to know Poland can win."

Chapter 40

One morning when the air is crisp, but not too cool, I find two large baskets by the door. "Walk with me today, Anna," Sophia says.

I pick up a basket and join her. We're off to see her friend Mrs. Tombola. "She's been too ill to come to church. I'd like to check on her." Sophia and I scoop up walnuts along the way. When we arrive at Mrs. Tombola's house, our baskets are full.

Her daughter, Verla, answers the door. She looks surprised, but not happy to see us. Sophia doesn't seem to notice. She barges in, bragging about the walnuts. I follow Sophia into the kitchen and stop in my tracks. Two soldiers are sitting at the table eating eggs and some sort of meat. They talk with each other, ignoring us.

Sophia clutches her basket tighter as if the soldiers might try to confiscate the walnuts. I can't move. Sophia turns to Verla and raises her eyebrows.

"They moved in last week," she says. Her words sound like an apology.

"Is your mother ill?" Sophia asks.

"Yes, this is her fifth day in bed."

Sophia instructs us to shell the walnuts and leaves to see Mrs. Tombola. Verla must pour coffee for the soldiers; one bangs his cup on the table repeatedly.

She pulls a chair to the corner of the room for me. After

waiting on the soldiers, she brings me a pile of newspapers, a kitchen knife and a big bowl. I start peeling the husks away from the walnuts.

I can understand a little of what the soldiers are talking about. They discuss their breakfast and the weather. One of the soldiers says he really likes the coffee and plans to hide it in his room so Mrs. Tombola and Verla don't drink it. The other soldier laughs and says, "A lot of good it will do you without a pot." At this the first soldier pounds his cup on the table. Their talk turns to numbers. Hundreds, thousands. Adding. Subtracting. I'm not sure if they are talking about their pay or taking over the world. I keep my ears on the conversation, in case they become curious about me.

Verla clears the table and brings a chair next to me. She reaches into the basket to pull out a walnut. Our heads are so close, the top of her head nearly touches my forehead. "One of them speaks Polish," she whispers. I don't say a word, but Verla chats. "Your hands have already turned brown. If I had some lemon juice I could clean them for you. It's been over three years since I've seen a lemon."

I have never heard of a lemon but I imagine it's some type of berry with lots of juice. Verla's nearly an adult so she knows a lot about life before the war. I fish another walnut from its husk and drop the husk on the paper.

Verla leans forward again. "I haven't had a soul to talk to and I must tell you something."

"What?" I finally speak, but it's only a whisper.

She whispers too. "When Mother fell ill, she fainted to the floor. I thought she was dead. The lanky soldier there, the one who speaks Polish, he lifted Mother and carried her to bed."

I glance at the soldier; he's tall and very thin.

"Then he ran straight for the doctor, all the way to town." Verla's forgotten about the walnuts. I reach for another. "He'd only moved in the day before. He didn't even know us."

The other soldier bangs his cup again and Verla rushes to serve him. The soldiers begin discussing their day's work. The tall soldier tells his friend, "I'm assigned to do a house-to-house search again with a few others."

"What this time?" The coffee drinker sounds bored.

"There's talk of a hidden printing press. Someone mailed another newspaper to headquarters. It's probably nothing."

Verla sits across from me again. I force myself to stay in my seat and work though I want to run to Sophia or home to Stephan. Verla is silent. I must be a perfect, unnoticeable child. I listen to every word, but the soldiers say no more about printing presses or house searches. Just as we shuck the last of the walnuts, Sophia finishes her visit.

When she walks into the room, I cover up my worry by smiling. "Perfect timing," I tell her. "We've finished all the work." I hold up my brown, sticky hands.

She actually laughs. The noise interrupts the soldiers and they look over at us. Sophia stands taller. "Gentlemen," she says, and nods like she is a proper lady. "Anna, run to the washroom and clean up. Time to go."

Verla excuses herself. I wash my hands quickly; I want to pull Sophia outside and tell her about the search. Verla and I step into the room at the same time. She offers me a red coat. I'm speechless.

"It will be cold soon," she says. "I've outgrown it."

I put it on. It fits perfectly.

Sophia thanks Verla and offers her a bit of advice. "You should make your home a little less inviting. Maybe the doctor can diagnosis your mother with something contagious?"

Verla looks alarmed.

Sophia shakes her head. "Not really, just enough to post a sign." She glances at the Germans. "Keep some people away."

Verla nods, speechless, and hurries us to the door. Sophia says under her breath as soon as we are out the door, "What makes them think they can live where they like? With a widow and her unmarried daughter, it's not proper!"

"She was nervous because one of them speaks Polish. He heard you."

Sophia smiles a bit. "I hope he did."

I motion for her to bend forward, and whisper in her ear. "I can understand German." I tell her about the printing press and the house-to-house search.

We run home, crossing the field to the back of the house. Sophia and I pause by the back door to catch our breath. The door is open and the voice of the tall German solider reaches us from inside.

"Sophia?" I'm nearly crying, I'm so afraid. I look up at her. Sophia's jaw is clenched and her stare is fixed straight ahead. I know what she's doing. The long pause isn't just to catch our breath. It is time to pretend, to act. I set my spine straight and give my mind a moment to settle into being the new Anna. But I can't be calm. On the streets, in Mrs. Tombola's house, in our very own home, everywhere we turn we see German soldiers.

Sophia takes a breath and reaches for my hand. She's ready. "Not a word, Anna. Remember, you know nothing." She steps through the open door. Sophia barely offers a greeting and begins sorting through the walnuts.

The Nazi soldier steps into the kitchen. He smiles when he sees me and wishes me a good day in German. I smile and answer him. I try to make my eyes unafraid and my face blank. I try to tell myself I know nothing. I hold my breath and count his footsteps on the wooden floor as he walks to the front door.

As soon as Stephan closes the door behind the soldier, Sophia pulls him aside and whispers in his ear.

He pulls on his boots and calls to Jerzy.

"No." Sophia shakes her head. "You can't take Jerzy with you this time. It's too dangerous."

"I'm not afraid," Jerzy insists.

"I know," says Sophia. "That's the problem."

"I need him. I'll be lucky to have three men on this short notice. We have to take apart that whole machine and hide it."

"I'll go," says Sophia. "I'll help."

Chapter 41

Stephan and Sophia are gone all day. The sky turns dark and they still haven't returned. I bring my books to Stephan and Sophia's bed. I want to know the moment they return and my room upstairs feels too far away. Jerzy's stretched out on his bedroll beside the bed, but I know he's not sleeping.

"What's the very first thing you remember?"

He's quiet for such a long time, I think he hasn't heard my question. "Horses," he says. I wait for more. "It's more of a feeling, I guess. The way the world moves past you when you're on a horse or in a cart. The height. When you're a child, there's only so much you can see until someone or something lifts you up. I think my earliest memory is that feeling of being up high on a horse—or a cart being pulled by a horse—and the world moving by step by step."

The way Jerzy explains his memory, I can almost hear the clip-clop of hooves and feel the to-and-fro of a cart being pulled.

"Sometimes," Jerzy says, "I'm not sure if I remember something for real or if I've only heard a story so many times that it feels like a true memory." He sits up and I can make out his form in the growing darkness. "My mother tells the story of the first time she left me in the cart in town. I was about four. When someone approached and asked about my parents I pointed to the two horses, calling one of them Mama and the other Papa."

I didn't think it was possible, but Jerzy has made me smile.

"What's yours?" he asks.

I think of Mama playing piano. The smell of wood in Papa's shop. Walking down the busy streets of Warsaw with my parents. Then I remember Jakub and the first game we ever played together. Another memory flashes in my mind, news about Jakub in Grandma's last letter. *Jakub has had a high fever for ten days and refuses to eat.* I swallow around the lump in my throat and push Grandma's letters out of my mind to answer Jerzy's question.

"Spitting apples," I say. "My cousin Jakub was—is—a year older than me. We used to fight about everything. When we were very young we even took each other's food. Our mothers said we'd pull the spoons out of the other's mouths. I don't remember that, but I remember the apples." I shake my head. "We'd chew up bites of apple until they were sticky and gooey and—" It's so disgusting; I can't believe I'm admitting this. "We used to spit the apple gunk at each other."

Jerzy laughs. "I was never that mean to my little sister."

Silence falls quickly around us and grows. I want to say something about Lidia, but I can't manage to make a sound.

"Let's rest now, Anna," he says.

"Yes, let's rest." I close my eyes and think of Lidia far away in Germany. I wonder if she's living with another family. This war is moving children around like toys on a game board. Maybe I'm only here because Lidia is gone. Stephan and Sophia must miss her so much. Perhaps that is the only reason they agreed to take a girl from the orphanage. Maybe Mama and Papa miss me so much that they found another girl too. Nothing in this war, nothing makes sense.

I wake between Stephan and Sophia sometime before the sun comes up. They're both sound asleep and reek of oil. Sophia's hair is sticking up. Stephan is sleeping in his clothes. There's something different about their faces when they sleep. Stephan's mouth is open a bit, he doesn't look worried at all, and Sophia's face has fewer wrinkles.

Jerzy and I let them sleep for much of the morning. He

checks the chickens and I tidy the house. When Stephan and Sophia finally wake, it feels like a celebration. I help Sophia scrub the clothes they wore last night. "Destroying the evidence," she says as we wring Stephan's shirt and hang it to dry.

For almost the whole day, I believe that we're safe, that everything is normal. But as Sophia and I peg the last of the wet clothes to the line, we see big clouds of gray-white smoke climbing steadily above the trees. "*Stephan*," Sophia yells.

He and Jerzy run outside.

We take turns keeping watch for hours, until the last of the smoke behind the trees disappears around dinnertime. Sophia insists we stay home. "We'll learn soon enough."

Stephan makes the rounds of our property every half hour, even after the sight and the smell of smoke have faded. At sunset he returns from watch holding a baby in his arms, with two small children trailing behind him. I recognize the children from the printer's house. The oldest says, "They got Papa and Mama." Stephan hands the baby to Sophia. He bends over the little boy who spoke, picks him up and sits him on the table. "Tell me everything," he says.

In a rush of words and tears the boy tells of how his house was searched. "They screamed about some papers in the cellar. They shot Papa. Mama pushed us out the door. She told us to take our baby sister and run. We hid in the woods. They shot again and left. Our house burned a long time. We waited for Mama but she didn't come out. Then we walked here."

Sophia gives the three children food and insists on taking them to town to their aunt and uncle. "We can't be associated. It's as simple as that."

They follow her without question. When the door closes behind them, I crumple onto the sofa and burst into tears.

Stephan sits beside me. "Anna, Anna." The tears won't stop. "Try to be calm."

"It's horrible. That man is shot. His wife is shot. Those children, the children." My words are lost behind my tears.

"In case someone comes, Anna," Jerzy says. "You really must be calm."

I stop crying long enough to look at each of them. They are dry-eyed and stone-faced as if orphaned children and murdered parents are nothing out of the ordinary. I want to ask them how they can pretend so well.

Stephan clears his throat. "I had fifteen people on that operation. Now two are dead. We all knew what we were doing, what we were risking. This is war, Anna."

Suddenly a flash of red burns in my chest and climbs up to my brain. "I know this is war. I know it! No one has to remind me about war! I—I never know what I'm doing. I don't know how to act with so many German soldiers around."

Stephan pulls me into a gentle hug. "That's the truth. No one knows what they are doing, not really. This blasted stupid war. You tell the truth, Anna."

Chapter 42

There's no need to look for paper. It's impossible to print the underground newspaper. The printing machine is in four pieces, kept in four different locations. Sophia insists it's too dangerous to try to put out a newspaper, and for once Stephan agrees with her.

For weeks after the fire, everything is quiet. Jerzy and Stephan leave in the morning as though they have real jobs. Sophia stands in the long lines for food. I check on the hens, clean the house and search for the poem.

The tall German doesn't visit, but Stephan and Sophia's friends come by each evening before curfew. I jump at first when people plow through the door without knocking and instead call out a greeting. After a few days I'm used to it, even expecting it. Instead of underground newspapers, people are spreading the news.

And the news is that the Germans are losing. They are retreating from the Soviets on the eastern front, being pushed out of France by the Americans, under attack by British bombers in Germany. Stephan actually lifts me in the air, as if I'm a small child. "The Home Army is pushing Germany out of Warsaw. They are really doing it."

This news is like a make-believe tale. One night after the guests have left, I ask, "Is it really true? Germany's the biggest country in the world. How can anyone stop them?"

Stephan and Sophia both speak at once. "They're not that big," insists Stephan. "Nearly all the rest of the world is fighting them," says Sophia.

Jerzy moves to the back door. "Wait, I'll show you."

He returns and unrolls a map on the table.

Sophia stands. "Jerzy, take that back. It's too dangerous."

Stephan is running his hand over the map. "No, Sophia. Anna has to learn. It's dangerous if people don't know the truth."

"If we're caught . . ."

"Didn't you hear her?" Stephan asks. "She thinks Germany's the biggest country in the world. It's what they want everyone to think."

Sophia nods and stands by the window, keeping watch.

"That," announces Stephan, "is Germany before September 1, 1939. And there's Poland and Czechoslovakia and . . ."

He's pointing so quickly and naming countries I've never heard of before. "Slow down."

Stephan patiently explains the map to me. *Germany isn't very big!* He shows me how the map has changed since the war started. Stephan is overflowing with information and so excited, it's like he's the teacher, not Sophia. "Look at this here." His finger traces a dotted green line. "France prepared, built a wall with underground bunkers all along the border. They had enough firepower to blow the Germans out to sea."

"Poland should have done that," I say.

"But it didn't work. Look what the Nazis did. They went into Belgium. Boom. Took the country in just over two weeks. Then waltzed right into France without any problems."

I shake my head. That's what the nun said in the orphanage. Germany always finds a way to win. They let you think you've outsmarted them and then they play a trick on you. Maybe they are doing the same thing right now, pretending to lose so they can waltz right back.

"It will really be over soon," says Sophia. "And then we'll . . .

we'll . . ." Sophia looks around to us for help. *What will we do after the war?*

"We'll get another cow," says Jerzy.

"And drink fresh milk every day," agrees Stephan.

A few days later, I am the first to wake. There's barely a hint of sunlight pushing its way through my window. I poke my head into Stephan and Sophia's room. Jerzy is curled up in a ball on the floor next to their bed. I listen to the music of their breathing. I take Sophia's sweater off the end of her bed, pull it over my head and walk outside. Leaning against the shed, I wait for the sun. I'm shivering. It's cold enough for snow. As I'm about to go inside for my coat and my scarf, a solitary figure wanders down the road from town. He's a soldier and he's walking quickly toward the house.

The printer was killed in a search because he saved a few newspapers. I remember Stephan's map. I know it is hidden in one of the sheds. I'm frozen between waking Stephan and Sophia and searching for the map to destroy any evidence. But the soldier doesn't turn to our house, he moves right past without even a glance in my direction. Before he disappears from sight, four more soldiers come into view. And more follow behind them.

I shout, "Sophia! Stephan!"

Stephan and Sophia burst out the door and stand beside me. Jerzy joins us a minute later. In that short time, the road has filled with soldiers all moving along in the same direction. Sophia holds her hands beside her head as if she can't believe her eyes. Stephan slaps his leg and says, "Those are the smart ones. They see the writing in front of their noses."

I ask Sophia what that means. "It means they know they'll be sent home eventually so they might as well start now."

I wish I could see the writing in front of my nose. As I stand protected between Stephan and Sophia, I wonder for the first time what I want my future to be like. I've waited so long for Mama and Papa. Yet now I can't imagine ever leaving.

Those first few soldiers were right. Each day, more soldiers leave. Many flash by in cars but some drive motorcycles. Two or three pass riding bicycles. Jerzy and I spend part of each day watching the soldiers leave our town, leave Poland. We stand next to the café across from the church. When I first arrived, I was afraid to walk down this street with soldiers sitting in the café, watching me. Now I am the one watching, watching them get out of town.

Jerzy's quiet as we walk back home, but I'm full of energy and words. "I feel stronger than an elephant," I say.

"Sure you do."

I walk backward facing him. "Really, I feel like I could wrestle a bear. I am strong. All of Poland is strong."

Jerzy turns me around and slings an arm around my shoulder. "I hope you're right."

After a few days, the roads are quiet. The neighbors and friends who stop by confirm it: there is not a soldier to be found in the town. I've dreamed of the end of the war at least a thousand times. In my imagination the war ends like this: the Germans are gone, people are dancing in the streets and Mama and Papa are running toward me. When they reach me they hug me tightly, even tighter than when I left them so long ago.

The next morning our house is full of people. They want Stephan to hold a banner and make a speech. I think it is to celebrate that the Germans are gone. He throws them out one by one.

"We should at least attend," says Sophia. "To get information if nothing else."

"I'll celebrate when the Home Army arrives. Until then I'm staying right here."

Sophia doesn't say another word, but she leaves the house following the neighbors. Jerzy and I go with her. The main street is lined with people holding banners. It's cold and the air smells like snow. It hasn't snowed yet this winter. People say that the new weapons the Germans are firing in Warsaw have made the ground so warm that snow melts somewhere between the clouds and the earth. I stare up at the sky, straining to see a single snowflake. The air freezes my face. I stand closer to Sophia and she runs her hands over my arms. It seems that snow would actually warm us. After almost an hour, a new army passes through town.

"They aren't German?" I ask Jerzy. A few people glace my way.

"No, Anna." He's gentle but his voice is impatient.

"They look the same. The uniform, it's the same color."

"Look at the details." Jerzy's voice is louder than it needs to be. "A bit of red somewhere on their uniforms, the collars or a band on the hats." I try to notice the red on the uniforms as the soldiers walk by. "Or you can look at the boots," Jerzy adds. "The boots are very different." Most of the soldiers march right past our town and on to the next; only a few stay. I study their boots, but they don't seem unique to me.

People visit all day, bringing bottles they have saved for years and offering toasts. But Stephan won't cheer. "The Polish Home Army should be here. When they arrive, I'll cheer."

His friends disagree. "The Soviets chased the Germans away. They saved us."

Even with all of the happiness around him, Stephan won't smile. "Yes, well, who will save us from them?"

After a week, I can't believe how much is the same: we still pray for eggs and rarely find them under our hens, we still sleep and rise at the same time. Also, we continue to line up for food. Some things are new: we no longer talk about the end of the war, because it is here. People are smiling and boasting, free to talk about anything. Almost anything.

Sometimes I hear Sophia's friends overcome with anger at how the Germans treated the Jewish people. Sophia agrees. She says it's terrible. When I overhear these conversations, I wonder if I should share my secret. With the Germans gone, it must be safe. But some of her friends say they are happy the Germans ran the Jews out of Poland. Then I hold my breath and pray that Sophia will stand up and argue. Though Sophia doesn't agree, she doesn't disagree either. She changes the subject. At night I wonder if Sophia ever met a Jewish person. I'm sure Sophia loves me. Still, I'm afraid she would love me a little bit less if she knew the truth.

Chapter 43

A few weeks later, I feel as irritable as Stephan. The end of the war was supposed to mean something. At the end of the war we planned to move the chicken coop closer to the house. But there's still not enough food, so Stephan and Sophia decided our chickens should remain in hiding. And they aren't the only ones hiding.

Stephan reminds me often that the war isn't really over. Though the Germans have left Poland, there is still fighting all over Europe and other places in the world. I examine a plate I just washed to make sure it is really clean. I can't concentrate on even the simplest tasks.

When the last dish is dried and put on the shelf, I fold my apron and rush out the door. I run across the cold fields. Winter is nearly over. I don't stop until I reach the tall pine tree. I climb barehanded, stuffing my gloves into my pockets to keep them from being torn or covered in sap. Soon I'm high in the tree, certain no one on the ground could spot me. I look out over the rooftops in the direction of Warsaw. It is a clear winter day, but there is so much I can't see.

I feel better with the German soldiers gone. Not completely safe, just better. In the ghetto, people—even children—were shot simply crossing the street. I wondered which of us would starve first, Papa, Mama or me. In the orphanage there was food, but not family. Here I have both food and a new family. Sometimes I feel like I'm not pretending anymore, like I'm really and truly Anna Karwolska. Other days, like today, I feel as if I can't keep my secret any longer.

Before I learned to swim, Jakub taught me to hold my nose, let out my breath and sink underwater in the lake by my grandparents' house. He invented a game where we sat underwater with our eyes open, staring at each other. The first one to blink lost. He always won.

I climb down from the tree and notice Stephan in his workshop. The door is cracked open. I knock and he says, "I need more time alone." I pretend not to hear him and knock again, this time louder. "Sophia, I will be out in—" He turns and sees me. "Anna, what is it?"

I take a step inside and close the door to keep the cool air out, but it isn't much warmer inside the small shed. Stephan's sitting at his desk writing a letter. "Remember you told me that Warsaw is far away?" He nods. "How long would it take to walk from Warsaw to here?"

He looks at me so long I'm afraid he will ask me why I want to know this information. Instead he scratches the side of his face and says, "About three days, four at the most."

I thank him and leave, pulling the door tightly closed behind me. I stand facing Warsaw and decide that Mama and Papa are leaving Warsaw right this very moment and they will arrive at Sophia and Stephan's home in three days, four at the most.

But four days turns into four weeks. And winter fades away. And flowers bloom in the fields. And four weeks turns into five and then six. We never did have snow.

Chapter 44

Stephan comes in for dinner after spending the entire day in town. At first I can't figure out what is different about his face, but when he passes the bowl of beans to Jerzy, I see it. A smile.

I know it isn't the food he's smiling about, a small plate of beans and no bread or even a single carrot to add to the meal. "What?" I ask.

"What?" he says. His smile grows.

Sophia and Jerzy join in saying "What?" and Stephan answers the same. I laugh because we sound like a group of silly children.

Finally, Sophia stands up. "Tell us what you know!" Her palms are spread on the table and the way she leans toward us makes her look fierce.

"I'd rather show you," says Stephan. "After dinner." We finish in no time. After Sophia and I clear the table, he says, "Leave the dishes."

Sophia and I exchange a glance and head out the door to join Stephan and Jerzy. Stephan whistles as we head through town and Sophia takes his arm. "What do you think it is?" I ask Jerzy.

"No idea," he says. "I hope it's a cow. Or even a rabbit."

We make it to town and cross the main street. Stephan heads right to the café, though I know we have no money for even a glass of water. He opens the door. The large room is packed with people. They are all quiet, listening to someone speaking at the front of the room. I look around but don't see the man who is speaking. Stephan lifts me so that I'm standing on a chair. Everyone is gathered around a big box on the counter.

"It's a radio," says Stephan. His smile grows. "They are now broadcasting a Polish station out of Warsaw."

I sit down on the chair and remember the large wooden radio in our home. Music played in the evenings. Once a play that Uncle Aleksander was in was broadcast live. And during the war, when Papa left to fight, Mama was glued to the radio waiting for news from the front lines. And when the bombs came, we made a tight circle around our radio—me, Mama, Grandma, Aunt Roza and Jakub—all day, every day. At night we slept in the basement and prayed the bombs would miss us. *I haven't even thought about a radio in years. And I used to listen almost every day.*

Weeks pass, and months. The weather becomes warm. Jerzy and I both need new shoes but we don't mention it because nothing has changed. No money, no work and very little food. The Germans are gone, but every day is the same as the next.

Cool spring rains fall for three days. I stand outside in the sprinkles after a downpour and look for a rainbow, but there isn't one. I gather my books and search for Sophia. I find her in her bedroom unraveling a sweater and rolling the yarn into a ball. She pats the bed beside her.

"I finished reading your poetry book. And the two I borrowed from your friend." She gives me a hopeful look. I shake my head. "I couldn't find the poem."

"I'll help you look, Anna."

"Maybe I've remembered it wrong. Maybe it was all a dream."

Sophia sets down her yarn and pulls me into a hug. "Never give up, Anna. I'm sure to have more poetry books. I'll start searching tonight right after supper."

A few days later, while I am washing the lunch dishes, there is a loud knock on the door. I freeze. Sophia stiffens. No one knocks around here. I stay in the kitchen washing the dishes as Sophia answers the door. "Yes?"

"I've come for Anna." It's a man's voice. The voice of a stranger.

Chapter 45

I place a glass on the shelf above the sink without making a sound. "I don't understand," says Sophia. I move closer to the living room, wringing my apron in my hands.

"My name is Mr. Goren. I'm from Warsaw. May I come in?"

Sophia races into the kitchen and nearly bumps into me. "Do you know a Mr. Goren?" Without waiting for my answer, she opens the back door and hollers for Stephan. He runs, barreling through the back door. "There's a man here from Warsaw," Sophia says. "He's come for Anna."

I walk between Stephan and Sophia into the front room. Jerzy follows behind us. Mr. Goren nods at me and turns his attention to Stephan. "I'm here for Anna Bauman, daughter of Henryk and Sara Bauman, formerly of Warsaw."

"There must be some mistake," says Sophia. "Anna's name is—"

"Karwolska, I know," says Mr. Goren. "It's an assumed name, a false identity."

They both turn to me. Stephan quickly looks up to the ceiling, but Sophia's eyes fill with tears. She's searching my face. I can't bear to look into those eyes.

I don't like Mr. Goren. I'm not sure what will happen to me if I leave Stephan and Sophia. Still, I have to know. I look at Mr. Goren. "My parents?"

Sophia lets out a sob and leans against Stephan.

"The important thing is getting you back to Warsaw," says Mr. Goren. *Why is getting back to Warsaw the important thing?* I've seen the photos in Stephan's newspaper; the entire city was flattened.

I gather my courage and ask, "Are my parents alive?"

Mr. Goren forces a smile. Really his mouth is just a thin line stretched across his face. "I don't have all of the details, but I'm only sent to find children who have family to care for them. So someone in your family has survived. We should leave immediately."

One, maybe both, of my parents are alive.

"You can't leave immediately," Sophia insists. "You must stay for dinner. Departing in the morning would be much better."

Mr. Goren stands stiff and straight. "It's such a long journey. As you can imagine, the roads are very bad. I'm sure Anna would prefer we leave at once."

"I've been ill," I lie. "It's not possible for me to travel today."

Mr. Goren joins us for dinner. It's arranged that Mr. Goren will stay in my room, Stephan will sleep with Jerzy in the living room and I will share the bed with Sophia.

Sophia helps me pack. Three drawers hold my clothes, the red coat and a few books. She places my things in the bag with flowers embroidered on the side. I trace my finger around a red rose, remembering how this bag helped on our secret mission for the newspaper. "The flowers are beautiful," I say.

"My mother made it," says Sophia. "I want you to have it." She sets the old school uniform in the bag. My mother's cloth is tucked into one of the pockets.

I follow Sophia to her room and she sets the bag next to her bed.

Lying next to Sophia on her big bed, I'm more awake now than I was when I opened my eyes this morning. I know Sophia's not sleepy either. She reaches for something beside her bed. "I have something for you. I just found this yesterday." Sophia passes me a book with a strip of cloth marking a page near the end. "Go on, open it."

I open the page to a poem: *To the Young* by Adam Asnyk. After glancing at the first few lines, I know it is the poem Papa said to me so long ago. I push the book to Sophia. "Will you read it to me, please?" I close my eyes as she speaks the words, strong words. We're both silent when she finishes.

I open my eyes and find Sophia's eyes locked on mine. "Perfect words for a new beginning," she says. I nod. My eyes are filling with tears. "Anna?"

I don't wait for her to say anything else. "I didn't break the eggs," I blurt out. It's a strange place to start. But I talk and talk. I tell her about Zina and Jozef. How I understood a few of their words. "I had to help them, to bring them some food."

She pulls me back so I'm leaning against her, and wraps her arms around me. Facing away, it's easier to talk, to confess. "Stephan got the letter from his sister. I was afraid you would all be shot. Because of me." I tell her about being Anna Bauman, in Warsaw, about Mama who played piano and Papa who made furniture. Sophia's clenching my hand, my fingers woven between hers. It's as if my words travel down my arm like electricity and flow from me into her. I tell her about the ghetto, about becoming Anna Karwolska. I don't stop until I've told her everything.

"I'm sorry," I say when I finish. I turn to face her. "I'm sorry I didn't tell you sooner." But that's not all I'm sorry about. There's something else crushing me. It's almost too big for words. "I'm sorry that I put you in danger. You, Stephan and Jerzy."

"Oh, Anna," Sophia's voice is scratchy from crying. "I wish you hadn't gone through this all alone."

My sobs grow stronger. "I'm sorry. I'm so sorry."

"Shhh, Anna. Please. There is no need to apologize. I'm not

upset with you. We knew. We all knew you were Jewish." She looks away.

"You did? How? Who?"

"The Resistance group that asked us to help you. They said you were Jewish and needed a home. When you came from the orphanage we just assumed you were an orphan."

"You knew?" Sophia's eyes dart all over the room before landing back on my face. "But why didn't you say anything?"

"You seemed, well, Catholic from the very start, the first meal, the first Mass. I thought maybe you were young and didn't remember." She takes a deep breath and lets it out slowly. "I've asked a few times, about your parents, but you never opened up."

These past two years could have been so very different. I could have been Anna Bauman here at home with Sophia, Stephan and Jerzy.

I let out a sigh and lie down. Sophia does the same. When I roll to my side, Sophia puts her arm over me. "Anna, you're like my very own daughter." I can tell Sophia's out of tears. She begins to breathe easily.

"Sophia? My parents are getting their daughter back after such a long time. I hope that Lidia's on her way home to you too."

"I hope so too," she says.

Chapter 46

Before Mr. Goren has finished breakfast, Stephan walks around the table and puts a hand on his shoulder. "We're not comfortable with you taking our Anna," says Stephan. My heart grows so big I think it will jump out of me.

Jerzy and I listen quietly as Sophia and Stephan question Mr. Goren. They want to be sure I'm safe, they tell him. In a few minutes, it's obvious that Mr. Goren is with the rescue organization. He knows everything about my family including the addresses of my grandparents in the Lodz ghetto and my aunt in Canada. Next, Stephan and Sophia ask Mr. Goren to bring my family here instead of taking me away.

"We'd like to meet them," says Sophia, "and to ask . . ." She looks up at Stephan.

Stephan clears his throat. "We want to help. We were actually hoping to adopt Anna when we thought she was an orphan."

Mr. Goren rambles on about paperwork and the Soviets and people moving around so unexpectedly in Poland. He ends by saying a Jewish child requires Jewish parents, as if Stephan and Sophia—who risked their lives for me—aren't good enough to be my parents.

I stand and clear the dishes from the table before he can insult them more.

Mr. Goren has a big black car. The fenders puff out over the wheels the way a woman's skirt billows out when she rides a bicycle. It makes the tires look small, too weak to carry such a huge amount of black metal. Mr. Goren shakes hands and climbs into the car. Jerzy hugs me fiercely. When we pull apart he holds his hand up and I match my palm to his. We don't say anything. He will always be my brother.

Stephan's next. "Write to us. Let us know if you need anything." While Sophia hugs me, Stephan walks around the car. He tells Mr. Goren to bring me right back if he can't locate my family in Warsaw.

"I'll write," I promise. I can't bear Stephan's sad eyes and Jerzy's faraway expression. "I'll come back to visit. I will."

Sophia walks me to the passenger side. Even when I'm inside, she keeps bobbing her head in the window like a mother bird checking on a nest. She reaches in the window for my hand, just as Mr. Goren starts the car. Suddenly I'm terrified to leave. I want to pull Sophia into the car with me. I don't want to let go of her hand, though I'm worried Mr. Goren will drive off and hurt Sophia. Sophia's not worried at all. She puts her whole head in the window for one last hug. "You'll always have a home here," she says.

I don't take my eyes off the three of them as we drive away. Too soon we are off the country roads and driving through town.

Mr. Goren is silent but glances in my direction every few minutes. Finally, he speaks. "I'm pleased to see that you were well cared for."

Well cared for? He doesn't know what he is talking about. I was part of a family. I was loved.

"Please tell me anything you know. Are you taking me to both my parents? Or . . ."

Mr. Goren lights a cigarette and rolls it between his fingers. The smoke stings my nose. "I'm not sure how much you know about, let's say, the end of the war. There were many deaths. Your parents were sent away."

"Where were they sent? When will they come back?"

Mr. Goren blows a thin trail of smoke. "They were taken

to a camp. I don't know how to tell you. The conditions were horrible there. Most people didn't survive."

Most people. "Well, some did, right? My parents, they are the type that would survive."

"It's impossible to know for sure with so many people moving around. But considering that the camps have been liberated for months, we are operating under the assumption that those who survived are already back."

He is avoiding my question. "Where are my parents?" I want to raise my voice.

"They are unaccounted for, presumed dead." He moves his cigarette to his other hand.

"But you said yesterday at least one of my parents was alive. You said I had family to return to."

Mr. Goren coughs. "Family, yes. Not your parents. I'm so sorry."

"My grandparents?"

"No, they didn't make it," he says.

"My Aunt Roza? My Uncle Jozef? My Aunt Halina? My Uncle Isaiah?"

Mr. Goren slowly shakes his head.

"My Uncle Aleksander?"

Mr. Goren blows puffs of smoke out of his nose and shakes his head again.

I name all eight of my aunts and uncles. Mr. Goren only continues to shake his head.

I can't control my voice. I'm yelling. *"My cousin Hanna? My cousin Emanuel? My cousin—"* I force myself to say his name. "My cousin Jakub?"

"Stop, Anna." Mr. Goren no longer pays attention to his cigarette. He chews his bottom lip and stares straight ahead. But I can't stop. There are more names. I say them all, the names of every single person in my family. Still Mr. Goren drives on, shaking his head. I pound my hand against the window. This can't be true. This is not true.

"Anna, enough."

"How do you know? How could you possibly know? You haven't met my family. You've never even seen my cousins. You don't know my father. You are wrong."

He finally turns his head to me. "I'm sorry." His voice is soft. "I wish it weren't so. Believe me. I am telling you the truth. It is my job to find someone to take care of you before I come for you. They went on the transport."

"No, they couldn't have." The transports. We called them actions in the ghetto. They would round up people, force them onto the platform and then into trains. Away. We always hid. We *always* hid. "My parents wouldn't have gotten on a transport."

"I'm sorry." His voice is soft as if he's really very sorry. "They didn't have a choice."

This cannot be true. I want to jump out of the car. I want to run back to Stephan and Sophia. They can help me find my parents. "Are you trying to tell me that no one in my family survived? No one at all?"

"Your father's sister in Canada. A Felicia Levison. She's been contacted. She knows that I left yesterday to retrieve you. She's waiting for word that you are safe."

My Aunt Felicia? She left for Canada when I was a baby.

I stare at the small farmhouses surrounded by fields, tiny sheds and barns. The world looks the same as it did yesterday. We pass a small gray farmhouse. A group of children chase each other outside. I can't hear them, but I can tell by the way they move that they are shouting, maybe even laughing. *How can anyone laugh on a day like this?*

Chapter 47

The road grows bumpy. My window is covered with dust. We are driving near the bank of a river. "Warsaw. This is Warsaw."

Mr. Goren slows the car to a stop. "What's left of it," he says. "No more roads. We walk from here."

I look across the river. Where once a city stood there is . . . emptiness. Flat. Broken. Warsaw now looks like a desert. A desert of concrete and trash and broken buildings. I can't resist walking closer to the river, though there's no longer a bridge to take me across. One building stands in the city. One building surrounded by rubble. "What is . . . ?" I recognize the structure before I finish my sentence: it's a Catholic church.

"We can't get any closer. Come this way." Mr. Goren turns his back on the ruined city.

I follow him. "Have you been over there yet?"

"Yes, it's been well searched. We even found survivors hiding in the rubble." I look again at the blasted-out buildings. "There's no easy way to get across," says Mr. Goren as if he can read my mind.

But there must be a difficult way to get across, because people are hard at work, clearing rubble, pushing wheelbarrows. I walk alongside Mr. Goren and in five minutes we arrive at a long two-story building surrounded by guards. "She's with me," says Mr. Goren to the guard in front of the door.

"Jaina! Jaina!" calls Mr. Goren as we walk in the door. A

162

tall thin girl speeds down the stairs to us. "Jaina, this is Anna Bauman. Please get her settled. She is to testify tomorrow. That is all." He turns and leaves without another word.

I stare into the girl's dark eyes. "Come with me," she says. Jaina leads me upstairs to a room with rows of beds. "You are number 86. This is for you." She hands me a washcloth and a green toothbrush. "Is something wrong?" she asks.

Is something wrong? A man, a stranger, took me from home. He told me that everyone in my family is dead. He walked me past a Warsaw that is bombed out, destroyed. Finally he brought me here to a guarded building where I don't know a soul. No, something is not wrong; everything is wrong.

"Why, I mean . . . guards?" My stomach is cold as if I've done something wrong. Maybe Mr. Goren brought me to the wrong place.

"It's nothing to worry about," says the girl, Jaina. "They're Jewish."

"But why? The war is over."

Jaina tilts her head and studies me a moment. "They protect us. They keep us safe. Don't worry, Anna."

I walk the halls and follow my ears to the crowded dining room. It's just like the orphanage but larger, and boys as well as girls. So many children of all ages. *Were all of these children in hiding like me?*

I search the noisy room for a familiar face, someone from my old neighborhood or the ghetto, even the orphanage. But I don't recognize anyone. I stand in line and I'm served soup in a tin bowl. Soup. There's always soup.

My arms feel heavy. It is exhausting just bringing the bowl to my lips. I drink the last drop of soup but wonder, *What is the point?*

Why did I become someone else? Hide in so many places? Leave my family? Why, if no one else survived? Why did I leave Sophia and Stephan to come here?

The other children are talking to each other. Some even talk to me. The words buzz around me but I can't hear anything. I force my heavy legs up the stairs and find bed 86. I'm so tired. I wind my face cloth tightly around my new toothbrush and fall into bed without using either one.

Chapter 48

A gunshot explodes in the night. The blast shakes the floor and the window. It sounds like it is right next to my bed. "Sophia! Stephan!" I start to call for Jerzy too, but I recognize the new room, the girls lined up in the rows of beds. Most have slid off and under their beds by now and I do the same. We scoot far back under our beds, close to the wall.

More gunshots. Breaking glass. Shouting. Horrible words fly through the air. Then footsteps and laughter as a crowd runs away. The girls climb back into bed and I do too. But I stare at the nearby window, wondering if anything will sail through it after I close my eyes.

After breakfast, I'm taken to a small room. A man with round wire glasses sits behind a tiny desk. "Name?" he asks without looking up.

"Anna," I say.

He lifts his head to look at me. "I see about a dozen Annas a day, you'll have to be more specific."

My heart races up to my head and booms in my ears. "Anna Bauman."

The man motions to the chair opposite him. I sit and see him scratch my name at the top of a blank piece of paper. "Anna, I'm going to ask you some questions. You must be completely honest." He begins with easy questions at first. How to spell my name. The names of my parents. My address in Warsaw before we were sent to the ghetto. Our address in the ghetto.

"What is your birthday?"

When I tell him, he glances up. "Tomorrow. You'll be twelve tomorrow."

A lump grows in my stomach. "I know."

He clears his throat and says, "I'm going to ask you the most important question of all and I want you to tell me every detail you can remember. Do you understand?"

"Yes."

"Tell me how you survived the war."

How can I answer such a question? It would take forever. "So many people helped me. It was over such a long time." I study my shoes. "I don't even know where to start."

"We're going to start at the beginning and just take it a bit at a time."

He writes quickly as I talk. At first I don't like talking about Mama and Papa, about leaving the ghetto. Somehow the scratching of his pen on the paper adds strength to my voice. Eventually it feels right, important, that I'm telling my story and someone is writing it down. When I get to the part about Martin and Frieda arriving at Auntie's house, there is a loud crash against our wall. "What?"

"Nothing," says the man. "Someone must have knocked over a chair."

But it comes again, even louder this time. It sounds like someone is trying to break through the wall.

We hear a boy's voice wailing. "I'm not under arrest. Let me out! Let me out!"

The man with the glasses walks around his desk and opens the door. A boy with red hair sticking out in every direction is kicking the wall outside the door. He looks to be about ten years old. "Let me out! Let me leave, you dirty Jew!"

Mr. Goren's voice fills the hallway. "Chaim, stop hitting the walls."

The boy screams, *"My name is not Chaim; it's Casmir. I am Casmir!"*

Mr. Goren's voice is cool and steady. "Chaim, come back in this room and sit down."

Chaim hits his head against the wall. "I am not Chaim. I am not Jewish. I'm a Christian. I'm a loyal German. I'm a Soviet. I hate all of you!"

"It's important that you sit down." Mr. Goren advances to Chaim and holds him by the shoulders.

"Let me go." Chaim kicks the wall. "Death to Jews! Death to Jews!" Mr. Goren lifts him in the air. But that doesn't stop Chaim from yelling "Death to Jews!" as Mr. Goren carries him down the hall.

The man with the glasses closes the door, takes his seat and says, "Where were we?" He looks up at me as if nothing has happened.

"That boy? Do they have the wrong person?" It's possible. The way children were moved so often, especially orphans. What if someone changed houses and Mr. Goren took the wrong child, a Christian boy?

"No, that's just Chaim. He learned to be Casmir when he was only four years old. And . . . how can I say this? He learned well."

It's cool in the room but my neck is sweating. I feel as if I could vomit.

"He's going to be fine, really," the man says. "Actually, he's a lot better than when they first brought him in. It's just a matter of time."

Everything is always a matter of time. A matter of time to grow older. A matter of time for the war to end. Adults really have no idea what they are talking about.

The man checks his watch. "Time for lunch," he says.

I hope he's at least right about that.

Before lining up for food, I search the faces of the children. I hope to find Halina and Marek or Sonia from the ghetto. I search for Martin and Frieda from Auntie's house. Everyone will be older. Even the baby, Rachel, whom we rescued in the crate; she would be three by now.

I poke my head into the room with the small children. "Is there a girl named Rachel here?"

A woman with dark curls pulls out a list. "No Rachel. Are you looking for your sister?"

I shake my head. "Not my sister, just someone I know."

I find a seat in the dining room at the end of a long table. A group of boys joins me. They look about my age, maybe a year or two younger. Two of the boys cross themselves and bow their heads. One mumbles a Catholic blessing. The other simply stares at his food.

It really is the end of the war. I don't have to keep secrets. I am surrounded by people who know I am Jewish, and I'm safe. I remember how Papa always blessed our food, any food, even a single carrot shared between the three of us, even scraps if that was all we had to eat.

"Wait," I say, before any of the boys takes his first bite. "Do you know the Jewish blessing?"

They stare at me wide-eyed. "Isn't it the same?" asks a boy with a sad face.

I shake my head. "The soup has vegetables. We would say 'Blessed are You, Lord our God, King of the universe, who creates the fruit of the ground.' "

"Say it again," asks the oldest-looking boy.

I say it once more and then we all repeat it together. "She's like a nun," says the sad-faced boy. He looks like the youngest of the group.

"Not a nun. She's like a teacher," says the boy next to him.

They talk about Chaim. "Chaim, Chaim, the crazy man."

"I can't figure him out," says an older boy. "His mother visits every day and he says, 'I am not your son. I'm Casmir.' "

I feel a flash of anger at Chaim. He has a mother and he won't acknowledge her!

"What are they going to do with him?" asks the youngest boy.

"Keep him here until he remembers who he is."

"What if he never does?" I ask.

Everyone shrugs.

Mr. Goren enters the room. He's walking with someone. The person is bald and so thin; I can't tell if it is a man or a woman.

"Levi," says Mr. Goren.

The boy with the sad face looks up. "Mama!" He jumps up and throws his arms around her, saying "Mama, Mama, Mama" over and over again until the entire room is quiet. Everyone is staring at the thin woman and Levi. But he doesn't seem to notice anyone else. His eyes are fixed on his mother as if he can't believe she's really here.

The other children scoot to give them room to sit. Levi looks up at Mr. Goren. "He told me you were dead."

My heart soars. Mr. Goren was wrong about Levi's mother. He could be wrong about my family too!

Mr. Goren sits down next to me. "I spoke to your Aunt Felicia last night. She's trying to make arrangements for you to come to Canada."

"Leave? When?"

"It isn't easy. Paperwork. Permissions. Could take months." He stands to go.

I don't like the idea of Mr. Goren or Aunt Felicia deciding my future. I've held onto being Anna Bauman through everything, for myself and for my parents. If I can't be with Mama and Papa then I want to be with my Polish family, with Sophia and Stephan and Jerzy.

I remember Papa, so proud to be Polish. "It's not one or the other, Anna," he told me when we had to move to the ghetto. "We are both Polish and Jewish." Papa standing by the window. "One hundred and twenty-three years Poland was absent from the map. Then back again. Nothing can stop the Polish people."

I stare at Levi and his mother and pray that someday very soon Mama and Papa will make their way back to me.

Chapter 49

Levi and his mother leave the room. Most of the other boys scatter too. Some older children fill in the places around me. They talk about their interviews, share their stories. Some girls say they were treated badly staying in homes and in orphanages. A brother and sister tell about living in the forest. They made their own fort and slept during the day and searched for food at night, even in winter. Two boys say they lived in the forest and fought with the Home Army.

"We had tents and bunkers," says the older-looking boy with a round face.

"And food," adds the younger boy.

I'm sure that's where Jerzy took Zina and Jozef. Stephan must have been helping the Home Army.

"How old are you?" I can't help asking.

"Fifteen," says the taller one with the round face.

"Sixteen," says the other.

A girl with large green eyes says she fought with the Polish army too. "There were lots of us girls fighting." She looks old enough to be a solider.

A boy with shaggy blond hair says, "I fought with the Ukrainian army."

We can't hide our surprise. "Impossible! Really?"

But the blond boy insists. "Anyone who was fighting the Germans was a friend of mine. And they had food, too."

I ask the question I'm sure everyone is thinking. "Did you really fight? In battles?"

They all speak at once. The girl with the green eyes speaks the loudest. "Sometimes fighting, but more often sabotage." Her voice is buzzing with energy. "We blew up train tracks, set Gestapo headquarters on fire and spied for the Home Army."

Her excitement is contagious. Everyone asks, "You were a spy?"

She nods her head. "Yes. Two girls in my group lived in town and worked cleaning for German officials. We met at the market every day. While we pretended to shop, they told me what they learned. I memorized everything and ran back to camp with the news."

"I heard about the fire at Gestapo headquarters," I say. "The family I stayed with printed an underground newspaper. I helped too."

Talk turns to the future. Many of the boys and girls around me are planning to go to Palestine. Their voices are full of excitement. Still, I bet that many months ago their dreams were the same as mine: the war would end and they could move back home and be with their families.

There is a lull in the conversation. It seems like people are looking at me. So I tell them. "I was six years old when the war started. That's the last birthday I remember being happy. I was nine when I left the ghetto and ten when I left the orphanage. Tomorrow I will be twelve." I swallow and look around. "And I have no idea at all about my future."

Chapter 50

A few of the people I spoke to yesterday remember and congratulate me on my birthday. But even when they sit near me, I am alone. In this building crowded with children, I am alone.

My cousin Ada turned twelve before the war. My mother and grandmother stood at her side. "This is your most significant birthday," they told her. I couldn't wait to grow up too.

I watch the children struck with the hunger. They bring their plates to their faces and shove food into their mouths with their hands. Not all children. Some, like me, have had enough to eat. Many of the girls and boys cross themselves before eating and mumble prayers that are not their own. My heart is overflowing with sadness and I can't blink back my tears. I'm filled with emptiness. I'm sad for everyone here.

In seconds I realize my tears are selfish. I'm crying for myself. After years of pretending to be one, I actually may be an orphan. After nearly two years as part of a family, I am all alone. After so long pretending to be someone else, I feel lost.

I miss Sophia. And Stephan. And Jerzy. It is true that they said I would always have a home there. Being Anna Karwolska meant being afraid. I was afraid to say the wrong thing, afraid to talk in my sleep, afraid of being caught, of being killed.

Now my name is Anna Bauman again. I spent so many nights trying to remember everything about being Anna Bauman. But I am not that girl. She had parents, grandparents, cousins. She had a home. She was very young.

This is *my* most significant birthday. It is time for me to decide.

If my mother were sitting across from me, she'd give me her advice. I can't imagine her talking to me the way she and Grandma spoke to my cousin Ada. About boys. About what to study in school. Ada was so grown-up.

If Papa were here, he'd ask for my opinion. "What now, Anna?" he'd say. I imagine Papa sitting across from me, tilting his head, waiting for my answer. I'm crying again. After such a long wait for Poland to be free of Germany, how can I move to another country? Canada. I know nothing about it.

I clear my plate, determined to find Mr. Goren. I knock on the doors lining the hallways, interrupting interviews, but he's not here. After I've checked every room I turn and find Mr. Goren walking toward me, a thin smile on his face. Beside him is a tall boy, a few years younger than Jerzy.

"Anna this is—" Mr. Goren starts.

I throw my arms around the boy without waiting for Mr. Goren to finish. He wraps his thin arms around me and crushes me in a hug. When we finally release I look up at his face. It's long and thin, topped with very short hair, but I'd know those eyes anywhere.

"Jakub!"

We make our way out the front door and sit on the porch steps. Guards are posted at each corner of the building. They nod to us. I grab Jakub's hand. He doesn't curl his fingers around mine automatically, so I place our hands together palm-to-palm the way Jerzy did when we said goodbye. Jakub's fingers are longer than mine, but he's so thin each of his fingers is a sliver compared to my own.

"We heard you were so sick. I was worried you had typhus, worried . . ."

Jakub smiles at me. "Sick? When?"

"Grandma wrote to us when you first moved to the Lodz ghetto."

Jakub studies our hands. "Oh. I'd forgotten about that."

"You forgot? She wrote you were sick with fever for ten days!" All this time, I carried the fear that Jakub had never recovered. And he doesn't even remember the illness.

"It wasn't so bad. Especially compared to what came after." Jakub doesn't wait. He tells me. My grandmother is dead. So is my grandfather. And Jakub's parents, Uncle Aleksander and Aunt Roza. And all of Mama and Uncle Aleksander's brothers and sisters and their husbands and wives and children.

I shake my head. I can't believe him. "How? How do you know?"

Jakub looks directly into my eyes. "That's what happened at the camp. I was there. I know."

I don't want to believe it. I've heard about the camps. When Stephan and Sophia's friends came over and talked late into the night, I heard about the horrible death camps. *My grandparents. They were so old. Why?*

Jaina stands behind us. "Jakub?" Her arms are full of supplies.

"Yes?"

"Here." She hands him a toothbrush wrapped in a cloth. "You are on the first floor, bed number 224." She walks back inside.

I study Jakub. He holds my stare. His face isn't exactly the same. It's thin. So little hair. It's as if I'm looking at him underwater at the lake near my grandparents' house and the Jakub I see is a bit blurry. I take a deep breath, but hold his stare. I don't look away, but I blink before he does.

"Mr. Goren says my parents . . ." I swallow and shake my head. "My parents were in a . . ."

Jakub looks down at the steps and says, "He told me they were in a camp."

"If we go to Canada and they come to Warsaw, how will they find me? Find us?"

Jakub studies the small piece of pavement between his feet.

"Over one hundred days since I walked out of the last camp. Every morning when I wake up, I have to remind myself that I'm no longer there, that I have a chance." He runs his hands over his face. "I force myself not to think about it, but I will tell you. Anything you want to know about the camps, I'll tell you."

I don't want to hear about the camps. I want Jakub to tell me that my parents are alive and when I will see them again. It can't be true that they are really gone. It can't be true. I try to speak but can't make a sound. I clear my throat. At times I don't know what I am going to say until the words make their way out of my mouth. "I have a poem that my father read to me the last time I saw him. And I have a very thin strip of faded cloth that my mother used to tie one of my braids."

Jakub looks up at me. He waits.

I shake my head and try to stop the words, try to stop myself believing that it is even possible. "That can't be all that I have left of Mama and Papa. That can't be all there is."

Jakub pulls me to his chest. He strokes my hair the way Sophia did. "I will help you, Anna. If they made it, I will help you find them. And if they didn't make it . . ." Jakub swallows. "If they didn't survive the camp, I will help you find out what happened."

I close my eyes and feel the slow rise and fall of Jakub's breathing. He didn't say what I had hoped to hear, but his words have stopped my tears. His collar bone presses against my cheek and his hand moves clumsily from the top of my head to the end of my hair and back again. I can imagine that I'm being held by Sophia or even Mama.

"And Anna"—Jakub's voice is thin, as if he's afraid his words will hurt me—"even if we don't find them. The poem and the cloth. That's not all there is."

I know that Jakub's right. Each night since we've parted, remembering my life with Mama and Papa has shown me that. Still, I'm crying again and this time it feels like nothing in the world can help me stop.

Author's Note

This book was inspired by Irena Sendler. Before World War II, she was a social worker in Warsaw, Poland. During the war, she was a spy who smuggled food, clothing and medicine into the Warsaw ghetto and smuggled children out. Even though her name doesn't appear in the story, the character of Irena is there (as Jolanta in the ghetto and as Mrs. Dabrowska at the orphanage). Irena arranged every detail of the children's escapes. She received money from the Polish government in exile; they dropped it from planes using parachutes. With the help of hundreds of collaborators, Irena Sendler and the organization Zegota saved more than twenty-five hundred children.

I first learned about Irena Sendler in 2004 and knew immediately that I wanted to write about her. I was excited to discover that she was still living in Warsaw and began to hope that I could somehow meet her. I applied for and was awarded the Kimberly Colen Grant from the Society of Children's Book Writers and Illustrators. This grant made it possible for me to conduct research in Warsaw, and the Jewish Historical Institute there accepted my request to research their archives.

In March 2005 I flew to Poland with my daughter, Alexandria, who was eight years old at that time. With the help of a translator, I read testimonies recorded by children immediately after the war. I met Irena's biographer, Anna Mieskowska, and also met Irena Sendler. When we stepped into her room, Irena reached her arms out to us, smiling. She saved greeting my daughter for last and kept her close to her side the entire visit.

I smiled and spoke in Polish. I was sure I had said "Hello, it is very nice to meet you" in the formal way I'd learned in my Polish lessons. But the translator translated my greeting. She and Irena spoke a bit and laughed. She told me later that I actually greeted Irena by saying, "Thank you and good-bye."

Irena told us that her greatest challenge with the rescue operations was convincing the parents to allow the children to leave the ghetto. She praised her friends who risked and lost their lives helping with the escapes, especially Eva Rechtman. From our conversation, it was clear that Irena never thought of herself as a hero. Instead, she focused on the contributions of others who helped her and the brave parents who gave up their children.

Irena also spoke against torture. She stated, "I am living proof that torture does not work." On October 20, 1943, Irena was arrested and held in Pawiak prison. She was tortured every day for three months, but she didn't give up any information. Irena was sentenced to death. At the very last moment she was rescued.

Even after she escaped prison and knew the Germans were searching for her, Irena continued her work saving children. She wore a wig, changed her address every day and sometimes used the alias Klara Dabrowska. Irena walked with a limp because of the torture she suffered in prison and was in pain for the rest of her life.

When it was time for us to leave, she put her arms around Alexandria and asked, "Aren't you going to take a photo?"

Irena Sendler lived to be ninety-eight years old. Many of the children she helped rescue reunited with her when they were adults. Some of the survivors became her close friends and visited her at her home in Warsaw.

Irena and I exchanged letters after we met. I shared with her my struggle to write about the child rescues when the children were in such dire circumstances. She wrote back an encouraging response: "There are humane aspects that are extremely important to developing values: helping to rescue a human being from his misery, necessary courage and an ability to disregard your own danger in order to save somebody's life."

Irena was, is and always will be my hero. Last year at a Days of Remembrance ceremony (a national day for communities to learn about and remember the Holocaust) I spoke about the people who assisted Irena with the child rescues. Eva Rechtman insisted on saving the children rather than being rescued herself. Anton drove a tram with hidden children for many successful escapes before he was caught and killed. Women risked their lives teaching children to speak Polish and say Catholic prayers in the safe houses. They found doctors to place quarantine signs on the doors of these houses

Irena Sendler, Angela Cerrito and her daughter Alexandria

in hopes that rumors of infection would be enough to keep suspicious neighbors away. There were German soldiers who agreed to let children slip past the guarded gates. Custodians left the courthouse unlocked at night. Friends provided forged documents. Doctors offered medicine to help babies sleep during their escapes. The

Polish government in exile funded the operations. Churches and orphanages protected children. Hundreds of host families cared for the rescued children. Friends checked in on the children and brought money to host families. These brave individuals are the reason Irena didn't consider herself a hero. How could she when so many people—practically everybody she knew—were doing their part to save these children?

TO THE YOUNG
by Adam Asnyk (1838–1897)
Translated from the Polish by Jarosław Zawadski

The brightening flame of truth pursue,
Seek to discover ways no human knows.
With every secret now revealed to you,
The soul of man expands within the new.
And God still bigger grows!

Although you may the flowers of myths remove,
Although you may the fabulous dark disperse,
And tear the mist of fancy from above;
There'll be no shortage of new things to love,
Farther in the universe.

Each epoch has its special goals in store,
And soon forgets the dreams of older days.
So, bear the torch of learning in the fore,
And join the making of new eras' lore.
The House of the Future raise!

But trample not the altars of the past!
Although you shall much finer domes erect.
The holy flames upon the stones still last,
And human love lives there and guards them fast,
And them you owe respect!

Now with the world that vanishes from view,
Dragging down the perfect rainbow of delight,
Be gently reconciled in wisdom true.
Your stars, O youthful conquerors, they, too,
Will fade into the night!

WITHDRAWN